Love Letters with Spelling Mistakes

a collection of short stories

Love Letters with Spelling Mistakes

a collection of short stories

Dr. Vaijayanthi Subramanian

First published in 2019 by Think Tank Books™, New Delhi
Website: thinktankbooks.com
Email: editorial@thinktankbooks.com

Dr. Vaijayanthi Subramanian asserts the moral right to be identified as this book's author.

This is a work of fiction. Names, characters, places and incidents are either the product of the author's imagination or are used fictitiously, and any resemblance to any actual persons, living or dead, events or locales, is entirely coincidental.

ISBN: 978-81-936204-8-9
Price: INR 225/-
Maximum retail price of this book listed is only for the Indian subcontinent. Selling price may vary elsewhere.

10 9 8 7 6 5 4 3 2 1

Acknowledgements

I thank my mother Shalini Srinivasa for lifting me up when I could not find a way to come back; My husband Subramaniyan for letting me live in my imaginary world, yet holding me with common sense and wisdom; Son Surya for letting me type on my lap top at midnights and being absent; Lovely sister Shefali for being an empathetic listener and companion, therapist, friend all in one. I survived because of you!

I thank my Sister Vaishali, truly a scholar of English Literature for having educated me on several occasions. I remain her student always!

Sincere thanks to my brother Skanda Srinivasa for reading my story union territory and exclaiming, *Why are you not pursuing writing?'*

Gratitude towards my teachers of medicine and Psychiatry for inspiring me, and those who listened, cared beyond all boundaries.

I thank Late Dr. R.L. Kapur who constantly encouraged me to pursue Psychiatry.

I thank and honor B. Jayashree and her team of actors of Spandana who taught me Stanislavsky and art of theatre, a truly humbling experience.

I would also like to thank my colleagues Dr. Aditi Singh, Dr. Virupaksha HS, Dr. Nirmala, Dr. Satish Rao and Dr. Nagamallesh & psychologists Sujatha, Harshitha, Mohan and Sridhar for being so supportive.

I want to thank Mrs Annie Chandy Mathews, my English teacher and publisher of *'Peacock's Cry'* and *'I, Me and Myself'*.

I also wish to acknowledge Agrahara Krishnamurthy for publishing *'Silent Flute'*.

I want to acknowledge Dr. U.R. Ananthamurthy for reading all my poems despite being on dialysis and encouraging me to write more.

Thanks to my patients for giving me a chance to help them and learn about my foibles and strengths. I also thank those who refused treatment and remained friends!

Thank you! Gaurav Sharma and his team of Think Tank Books for being so prompt & professional.

Finally, I would like to thank my readers for picking up this book and reading me!

About the Author

Dr. Vaijayanthi Subramanian completed her MD in Psychiatry from the National Institute of Mental Health and Neurological Sciences. She is currently working as an Associate Professor of Psychiatry at MS Ramaiah Medical College, Bengaluru and consultant Psychiatrist at Indian Institute of Science, Bengaluru. She has worked extensively with survivors of child sexual abuse and published papers in peer-reviewed indexed journals. She has conducted several workshops in sensitization about abuse at Bengaluru, Mysore and Colombo at Sri-lanka.

Dr. Subramanian has been a professional expert of psychiatry on local TV channels, Chandana, Suvarna News, Samaya, Digvijaya, Udaya etc. and on FM Radio. She is multifaceted, having dabbled at theatre, a Bharathnatyam dancer and a musician.

Some of her poems were published in two anthologies *'Peacock's Cry'* (2006) and *'I, Me and Myself'* (2009). Her book *Silent Flute* (2013) was published as a part of Navodaya program to encourage Indian English writing in writers below 40 years by Kendra Sahitya Akademi, carries an eloquent foreword by late Dr. U.R. Ananthamurthi.

1. the union territory

~~~~~~~~~~~~~~~~~***~~~~~~~~~~~~~~~

Anu woke up later than she had intended. Bright coastal sun rays seeping into the room through the chiffon blue curtains rendered a blue halo to every object in the room. As she squinted her eyes to accommodate the blue light, the unfamiliar scent of strawberries assailed her nostrils. She was rudely dragged from that cozy lazy morning slumber where one dreams that one is asleep.

It was an air freshener used by the hotel staff. The scent of strawberries on a tropical coast like Pondicherry was incongruous. She was wide awake with this thought. As though she was recalling a dream, she recalled that she had travelled from Bangalore all alone to this city and to this hotel. What had seemed so right in that crowded hostel of Bangalore amidst cheerful chatter of students with "going home after exams" syndrome did not seem so right in this bright morning sunlight as the day yawned before her with no agenda. Getting away was all that she cared about while she was there, now that she had arrived she had no clue what to do.

She curled in the bed in the pose of a fetus feeling utterly foolish about her decision to come here, alone. Then she heard the murmur of the sea, wind howling outside, her skin rippled in goosebumps, responding to the talk of the sea. Missing the last exam of her engineering course was not her fault, he was to be
~~~~~~~~~~~~~~~~~

blamed. It was not foolish coming here, walking away from all that unpleasantness she concluded.

She wearily looked at her suitcase standing alone in the corner of the room, with its maroon hue looking odd, in the blue room. Shabby, overstuffed were the words that entered her mind making her feel self-conscious as though she had entered a party hall with an ill-dressed man. This unwanted association of her mind made her get down from her bed, put the case in the cupboard of the hotel and shut it close.

Sagar would have searched for her in the hostel, called all her friends by now, she mused. For the first time since she woke up, she smiled. She was even faintly excited like the hiding child in a game of hide and seek. She could imagine her friends standing up like exclamation marks, a second time in the same week. The first time would have been the day of the last exam that she missed. That morning she was in the Vishveshvarayya museum eating peanuts. She was unpleasantly aware of the relentless movement of the hands of the huge clock on the wall as it passed all the minutes and hours of the exam with no awareness of those who stood still. Like the concentric rings of the web of a spider, the minutes and seconds swirled their trail in her mind. The pendulum of the clock looked similar to a gold medal dangling.

Someone knocked on her door. There was a waiter asking, 'Do you want hot water, Madam?" She nodded. 'One or two buckets?' He peered inside, curious to see what kind of a man she was with. She recalled the receptionist looking behind her for a male figure last night. When she announced her name to be Miss Anasuya Pundit he was irritated with the 'miss' as though it spelt trouble. When she collected her keys and was moving towards the lift he had said as an afterthought, "no visitors after ten 'o'clock madam." She was too sleepy and also a wee bit scared to protest, so had weakly moved on. Now she said emphatically "one bucket only." She left the door open.

Pushed aside the curtains, to have the first glimpse of the sea. Behind two rows of shops, it looked like a silver zari bordered blue tissue sari like the one she would want to wear for her wedding reception.

She resisted her urge to call Sagar. Now that the exams were finished, she could react to his words, apart from reacting to the fact that she had missed her exams and had to do them all over again. When his tongue was in her mouth it could sense third moisture he had said. She felt like she was stripped in a market place, the first time she heard his words. Could she redream her dreams? Was there a second attempt possible in that subject? She felt drained, lacking all energy. Her eyes wandered to the corner of the room where an ornamental cactus was growing in a stained blue glass container. Thorns grew in the dark, they even looked pretty and their existence was justified when they were kept in blue glass containers.

She bathed in the hot water, vaguely insecure without her clothes even in the privacy of the bathroom, away from her home town, alone in this hotel. Could she survive a day here, she wondered? She quickly dressed in her blue jeans and a green top, a touch of the pink lipstick and she was locking up the room and all her private thoughts, walking out boldly as though a world was waiting eagerly for her company.

She reached the beachside restaurant by walk. It was deserted and desolate. The empty restaurant looked inviting as she was alone too. She ordered coffee and sandwiches. She ate them silently and sipping her coffee picked up a newspaper to do the crossword. The first clue was 'A bit of hope, a pet can invigorate' (3, 2). She looked at the second clue, 'They can be hard to lose, perhaps at golf' (5). She wrote 'holes'. The next clue was 'Were to pray that a fellow gets a bit of help' (6). This was easy, she wrote 'chapel'. Solving the third word made her go back to the first one. The word 'hopes' made her feel somewhat lonely or were it the 'pet'? A loud male voice said, "The answer is pep up." She looked up startled, into the blue eyes of a blond guy.

"If you don't mind can I join you?" His accent was local, despite the blue eyes, his skin seemed Indian somehow. He laughed sitting down and said, "There came a big spider and sat down beside her." She smiled back, the second smile of the day. He said, "I am Dhruva, born to an Indian doctor and a certain wandering French spirit. Although I was raised entirely by my Dad, I am condemned to remember my mother each time I look in the mirror." She had to introduce herself or else it would be rude. "I am Anasuya, an engineer from Bangalore."

"Why are you alone here? Is it to visit the Auroville?" She wanted to say she was not alone; instead, she was surprised to hear herself say "What makes you think I am alone?"

He looked mischievous saying, "I have a German Shepherd who smells when a sheep has strayed from her herd. She has taught me a thing or two about lonely persons, like doing crosswords in a restaurant." Then he showed her his copy of the same paper in which most of the words were filled." I am an old patient of the same illness."

"So that was how you knew pep up…" He laughed aloud. He was attractive, it could grow on her with time, it had happened before. Now he was new, he could only charm as hurt came later after one is sufficiently addicted to the charms. As she got up to leave, he followed her. "Are you going near the sea, I will come with you". She was comfortable with him, hence let it be. It would take far more energy to withdraw.

The beach was deserted except for a bunch of boys playing Frisbee. They found a place close enough and sat down at a respectable distance from one another. The sea appeared quite like her fears in the morning light. The laughter of the boys at a distance exaggerated the silence here between them. She felt no compulsion to touch the impeccable sheet of silence between them. With friends, she was acutely uncomfortable with silence, as though they could hear her uncensored silent thoughts if she did not speak, as if silence insulted friendships.

With a stranger here, the silence was soothing as if it was in its lawful domain. She watched the waves rising so high as though to reach the sky and then bending backwards, breaking into midgets, as if someone slapped them. At the furthest point where the ocean and the sky met she could still see a margin. Boundaries existed even there, and then was there no union?

When she had first met Sagar she had sensed intensity, a depth which bordered on violence, it had excited her. It was like the first trip to a foreign land. She was curious about that terrain; slowly it had grown up to be an addiction. He was defending felons, murderers but was unable to defend himself against the growing sense of alienation and despairing loneliness. He spoke to her in his inner voice which was so gentle and troubled like a sleepy baby that it clashed completely with his sure of men and matters demeanor of a criminal advocate.

When did the margins fade, she had no clue. While running down the stairs up to a point there was a choice, later the momentum kept on going and if she stopped she would fall. Like now she felt sore all over she didn't know where it hurt. He owned her, infiltrating into her thoughts and emotions, intangibly like the fragrance of an incense stick. It had made her feel important, grand and holy somehow. She only noticed the ownership when the final task of fencing had begun and fled. The waves touched her sandals soaking them wet. The sudden cool wet touch tickled her to smile like the lick of a puppy. Dhruva smiled too.

"Whoever said still waters run deep forgot about the sea." "Yeah touching you without permission tch… tch!" She chose to ignore the obvious hint. There were no shortcuts to intimacy. Boundaries must be respected, at least to begin with. Manners, decency, approach… all those frills disappeared quickly enough. Falling in love was a heady, intoxicating experience. Every place seemed empty bereft of him. And she felt like a garden in full bloom when his warm glance appraised her. That intense longing to dissolve in his arms flashes of being all mouth and hands entwined and the sweet illusion of being Siamese souls.

Then sleep was also an unwanted guest as it obliterated his presence. But retaining that initial magic and weaving it into the lacklustre fabric of everyday life was the difficult part. How much to give and how much should be kept for oneself, who is there to guide this? Recipe books told how many spoons of sugar and how many litres of water. To make a relationship sweet how much should be given? What proportion of time and how much emotion? Then there was this entity called 'self' nebulous, still refusing to blend. Who is he to define me it said, rebelling when limits were set. Why isn't he holding me, it cried when the trespasser left the territory?

She started to draw a circle in the sand with her forefinger, around herself. The waves erased it. She started to write words. She wrote "spark", the waves erased it. Then she wrote "margins", waves erased it again. Then she wrote "intimacy", next it was "possessiveness". When it was erased she was suddenly aware that Dhruva was looking too and turned to look at him. He was fiddling with a sea shell and intentionally seemed disinterested, avoiding her eyes. She was disturbed by this evasion, as she looked back at the sand she saw a crab inching its way to her. She let out a cry and with a reflex movement withdrew her legs.

Dhruva laughed at her throwing his head back, she was annoyed. "So possessiveness came back looking like a crab." She was nonplussed, it had not occurred to her. She looked at him with fresh respect.

"Don't you want to know what I do with my life?" She just nodded encouragingly and he continued, "I am an intern at JIPMER. In this hot city, it is cool to have doctor father's shadow." There was some story there she knew, a vulnerability aching to be undressed, a mask asking to be unveiled. What was that about French spirit, condemned to remember mother, a lonely German shepherd, he was being morbidly maudlin, but why with a stranger like her? Or was it all easy with a stranger? How can strangers redeem what friends could not? She forced a tepid reaction. He could connect clues and arrive at solutions, she couldn't care less she told herself to learn indifference.

"I have an entrance test for PG course coming up next month, so I and my study pal Dilip are cramming for exams, some days we have had enough and take a break." She remembered Shashi, if only she had studied on her own maybe she could have taken her exams. Shashi was a walking talking library with no index or organization. She quickly read up all topics consulting the library and in return organized it. Shashi evinced very little interest in her personal affairs and that was an advantage as it provided the hygiene and serenity needed to pursue their studies, a mutual interest. When the questions which they expected appeared in the papers they waved to each other across the exam hall. She had this habit of reading only what she liked, which he corrected forcing her to read the topics which she hated. It was a simple partnership of mutual convenience.

Sagar was furious when he discovered that she was spending her days and nights with this "Shashi" who has gender-ambiguous in his name, was actually a male. He had accused her of purposeful deceit. Every action had an equal and opposite reaction and she walked out of her exam. To her Shashi was not a male, he was a 'mind', full stop. But why was Shashi giving her surreptitious glances and smiling so foolishly in front of Sagar? Sagar knew her well enough to know there was no spark between them as far as she was concerned, but it was resentment against all that excluded him finding its voice. In her zeal to share her childhood, adolescence and every minute she had spent without him before he came into her life, she had unwittingly torn out the feathers of that fragile bird called love.

It sure couldn't fly now but would it die? Would it become a pretty feather, a dead appendage of a live wing between the pages of her book of poems, to be gazed at wistfully on a rainy night? She had some dried up flowers staring at her sadly amidst those pages already.

"Hey what did I say to cause so much Pathos?" Dhruva was looking at her with concern. She did not know that she was so transparent. She could not regain her composure, instead, she meekly muttered, "I missed the last of my engineering exams." Dhruva was silent for a while. She had expected him to make some ineffectual 'pep up' remark instantly, so looked up at him straining to hear. She had chosen to ignore every clue in his shadowy speech.

Now, it was his turn, as she was recovering from the embarrassment of having spoken too much or having spoken out of turn he spoke softly.

"Was it because someone died?" his voice was almost a caress. She swallowed hard a lump of self –pity, clinging to her vocal cords, clasping her words in its fist.

"Nothing as final as death."
"Well, you had me scared the way you said it. You are a professional, so you know you can take it again unless you were a gold medal aspirant, are you? You don't look like that tribe."

"Why? Because I don't have an oily plait?" "Yes. Plus members of that tribe don't miss exams even if someone died." Now she truly laughed straight from her heart. She had that familiar feeling of wonder which she had experienced standing in a restaurant on the top floor of a skyscraper called 'Top café' in Bangalore. Each tree looked like a bonsai from the top; each car looked like a beetle. People on the roads and pavements seemed minute like members of an anthill, and she was a part of that anthill. Ants had some problems, small ant problems!

The sound of the waves as they shattered at her feet and were reborn at a distance was like a song. Suddenly, she felt light-hearted enough to befriend the whole world, in that impulse she asked, "Where is your mother now?" She owed him that much curiosity.

He narrowed his eyes clearing a frown on his face said, "Emma is her name. Mother is someone who mothers you, and she never did that, to me at least. So I never call her that. She was a poet. She came to Auroville after reading "Savitri" of Aurobindo, maybe she was a pilgrim, unaware of her religion. She fell ill with Typhoid. My father doctored her and nursed her. As the fever raged in a step ladder fashion so did their love. If love isn't eternal what's the point? So my father grandly tied the knot. I was born before the first anniversary. And Emma's ex-lover arrived. My unsuspecting father housed him. Within a month of his arrival, she left along with him leaving me behind. Fortunately, here in India when mothers leave grandmothers to arrive. So I was brought up by my *Pati* (granny) who gave me a heavy dose of Sanskrit shlokas and scriptures to purify the wayward French blood flowing in my Indian veins.

But apparently, my father became a shadow of his original self after Emma left. He comes through for his patients but I look too much like Emma, so he looks at me tenderly from a distance. He never looked at another woman. He still treasures her parting gift, a bottle of Je Reviens perfume. It means 'I shall return' in English. Hunger is not romantic to the hungry. Fear is not so thrilling when you are the one who is afraid. So I don't find all this romantic. I have repeated this several times to many friends so don't get carried away thinking this to be intimate confidence delivered to your ears alone."
Anu corrected her over the sympathetic face into a more suitable nonchalant one. She saw a fisherman's boat spreading its net further away.

Was it possible to go back to a relationship that was discarded years ago? Like wearing an old discarded dress, it may not even fit. It was cast away on valid grounds which would remain the same she thought. What if grounds changed? But time would have been lost too, how to amend that? After the moments passed can they be retrieved? Love was lucky if it was not tested if ever it was tested and failed the test, there was no re-exam there.

She thought of Sameer and the feeling of confusion returned. In the pre-university college dissection hall, she had spoken to him for the first time. As she pinned the dissected mouthparts of cockroach with the sticky haemolymph on her hands she had to speak, she needed a parallel experience to distract her attention from the sticky cockroach. As she mumbled something to express the yucky feeling welling up inside her, Sameer had said aloud, "I thought the cockroach spoke to me for a second." She had giggled a little more than necessary, perhaps. They spoke while carrying out chemistry experiments, at first a mere grumble about this or that lecturer.

Then they played *anthakshari* of old Hindi film songs. Later some ghazal cassettes were exchanged. He told her silly jokes about the *Sardarjis* and sent her to peels of helpless laughter. Then he looked at her with immense self-congratulatory satisfaction mixed with longing, leaping out of his eyes.

It made her veins throb. As she hung around with a gang of girls who pretended they were above the laws of nature and felt absolutely no attraction towards the members of the opposite sex, it would mean an act of ultimate betrayal to talk to Sameer outside labs where her friends would be present. Besides, she was too proud to show any obvious interest. Then on the day of Holi she was pouring over some books in the library when Sameer came to warn her that senior guys were carrying colors and were mauling every other junior girl in the pretext of applying colors. He helped her jump over the compound wall and escape. She recalled his warm strong grip and the unmistakable smile of relief writ on his features as he watched her outside the compound wall. She had hesitated to hold his hand for a fraction of a second but the fear of being caught had overcome that. Implications of that chivalrous act were strong and undeniable.

He had kept a watch on all her movements in the campus and did not want another guy to touch her. From then onwards, his mere presence in some corner of the class filled her with warm vague anticipation. And the days he was absent despite all her friends being present, she felt the classes were not worth attending. At last, he asked for her phone number and suddenly home seemed an exciting place. She monopolized the phone much to the irritation of others at home. The cordless seemed to sleep with her in the nights.

Sameer did not allude to that emotion as love either. Thinking back she found it funny, but then she was scared to use that word if it were to spoil all that was there. As though naming that feeling stripped it of its uniqueness. Then they were lost studying for the second year pre-university exams. He was her alarm ring early mornings and the goodnight bell in the nights.

In the farewell party organized by juniors, she had worn a deep blue silk sari and they managed to meet behind the compound wall. Threatened of being parted forever made her cry and suddenly his arms were around her, his autograph book slipped. Before she knew his lips were on hers, his tongue urging them to open. No, their noses did not clash, he seemed to be an expert. This was not misty or intangible like a ghazal or a poem. It had taken them centuries to meet, and for that kiss from the centre of his universe to happen.

He scored an abysmally low percentage in the CET and she scored a state rank, making her college proud. He was devastated when she walked into the best engineering college in the state. His phone calls became less frequent. He once asked her if she was ashamed of him and when she consoled he found it condescending. She felt like the flower of a touch-me-not plant that closed up even for a caress. She was powerless to alter its misplaced withdrawal reflex. Knights in shining armor were almost as vulnerable as damsels in distress or even more so.

Then one fine day she heard from a common friend that he was engaged to marry a girl from Saudi Arabia whose father sponsored his medical education abroad. She was left with the memory of that one kiss lingering like a lone pearl with no hope of becoming a part of any jewel. Telephone groaned a couple of times before taking its final breath. Unspoken promise sealed by a kiss was broken. She began to mistrust silences. Nuances were no longer appealing.

The space between the lines was often empty. Unsaid truths became lies easily.

One day while talking about the history of a scar on her knee she was carried away by Sagar's compassion and spoke about Sameer. When an ominous silence ensued she realized something was horribly wrong. Sagar had asked her what if Sameer had remained single, what if he had waited for her and wooed her, and what then? She did not know, maybe she would have outgrown him. After all, she had out beaten him. Was she too chauvinistic expecting the man to surpass her in all arenas? Why is it that her man must be taller, smarter, older, and braver always? Is love a conditioned response to a specific set of stimuli? She knew in her heart that if Sameer had not left maybe she would have. Somehow, her percentage had erected an invisible wall which was taller than the compound wall of their college.

She thought Sagar had to know every little thing about her. Was she wrong in resurrecting the past? What had started as a confiding narration metamorphosed into a guilty confession of some sort? One of those days when a butterfly turned in to an ugly pupa. Little chinks in their perfect togetherness blinked, nights seemed long and silent.

They were no Siamese twins after all. The kiss had affected him far more than anything else. Why were men so territorial in their affection? Why was her body his territory? How could she have been loyal to him before she even knew him, before she even knew that he existed? That stupid déjà vu feeling that she knew him before she actually knew him evaporated like dewdrops in the Sun. It was like a stench of spoilt flour between them. How to clear the air? She had thought to share the past with him, somehow made him a part of it too. But he was holding his nose, everyone disapproved of pasts other than their own. Why?

Loves me, loves me not tearing out the petals of a flower, how futile that was! She had thought love was the end and they happily lived ever after. No one had told her even after that there would be loneliness. She knew now, despite being loved by one another both felt the familiar pangs of unrequited love.

No, she could never go back to Sameer, ever. Memories were burnt, last rites performed, even the ashes were submerged. She was more like a central nervous system, all or none phenomenon. For her, all endings were bad and if it weren't, they wouldn't end at all. She could never do what Emma did.

Dhruva called out a child selling puffed rice. He seemed to know this kid well as he chatted with her about her father's drunken brawls. They bought two packets of puffed rice. As she was about to eat hers, a strong gust of wind blew it out of her hands into the ocean. The crisp rice flakes grew soggy in front of her eyes. Dhruva laughingly offered her his packet.

"Today the ocean is playing games with you, unwilling to swallow your possessive lover, willing to swallow your puffed rice." Anu was flustered. He seemed to connect clues more aptly than what she had given him credit for. For one long moment they looked into each other's eyes, he was daring her to speak. This was that bold moment when strangers invited friends. The recent hurt banged on her doors.

"When someone is jealous of your past what can be done? To exorcise ghosts is not easy. When the most benign of them can rock the ship, how to deal with the rest?"

"Who did the séance then? Who called the ghost?"

"I did." He threw away the shell in his hands into the ocean.

"Was that disclosure a test of some sort? Were you testing the waters?"

"Frankly I don't know. I wanted sympathy I guess." Dhruva looked at her strangely for a second and then laughed, roared actually. She was annoyed at first, slowly became angry and later livid fortunately he stopped just then. He asked her to remove a flake of puffed rice sticking to her nose, while she wondered confusedly if this had made him laugh he said, "You wanted sympathy for having loved someone else? What, did you expect an embroidered handkerchief?"

She was crestfallen by this revelation. Looking at her state he said more gently, "Why did you miss your exams, it was connected to this right?" "He did not express his anger towards the ghost or me for having brought it up instead he abused an innocent friendship, a pure partnership for studies and I lost my cool, I was not in the frame of mind to face a viva voce."

"He is right it is difficult to picture you in any pure, innocent friendship." Anu was angry again. "You don't know me at all, how can you say this?"

"Sorry, but you wear your vulnerability on your sleeve like an accessory. Is that called femininity? Maybe that is the right word. Like for example, when I saw you at the restaurant you seemed fragile almost like a child accidentally left alone by a careless parent."

"If I am allowed to be honest, isn't that you? A child accidentally left alone by a careless parent?" Now it was his turn to be angry she thought. But he was defenseless; she carried abstract knives designed by her strong feminine tongue. He had no right to refer to her femininity she thought indignantly. He looked sad as he said, "Maybe that is why I can identify them so easily, and connect." Anu simply nodded.

"When all your lover wanted was some reassurance, protective cuddling, and a couple of little white lies such as, *no one matters more than you, I can't live without you, he never made me feel the way you did etc… etc.* What do you do? Bang! Walk out of your exams and recreate a situation where he has to be sorry, on his knees all over again, protect you, what do I call that? You wrong yourself, just so that you can blame him. And then disappear like Cinderella, I am sure you did not even leave behind a glass shoe."

Anu's eyes were clouded by a thin film of tears. He was too clever he made her feel weaker by the minute. Did he mean that what he felt for her was not pure and innocent friendship? Suddenly, she was conscious of her green top clinging to her, and her legs not pedicured or waxed for months because of her exams. She could not recall how she looked in the mirror this morning. She looked at his hands with their long delicate fingers making a paper boat in the newspaper used to keep puffed rice. She was shy of a man only when she was attracted to him. Why was she resorting to 'femininity' every time she was made to feel powerless by an adversary? Why was she playing a pawn in every game of sexual politics?

"Why are you making that boat? It won't survive the ocean." If he did notice her subterfuge, he didn't make a spectacle of it. "It is a piece of art, not always useful, is made nevertheless. Its motto is the expression that is all. Want it?"

She took it from him and as an afterthought put it in her handbag. She was fond of useless mementoes. Reminders of rare occasions when her vulnerability met with indulgence.

"I guess I will do some shopping, my bus to Bangalore starts at nine at night, and so I will go back to the room and get some sleep." He was thrown off guard or did she imagine it? He didn't seem ready to bid farewell, "Can I come with you?" He looked hesitant and shy like a small boy asking for another piece of candy after the first one was given freely already.

"For shopping? Yes definitely!" She agreed. They walked silently to the row of shops which looked bright with colorful handicrafts and chiming Chinese wind chimes. She walked into a shop with aromatic candles in various shapes, sizes and colors. There was a glass bowl of water with rose petals floating and two flower-shaped candles floating. They were lit and shed a soft glow. As she smiled with pleasure looking at them, she paused to look up in the mirror to see Dhruva looking at her intensely with his arms folded across his chest. She averted her gaze and chose some candles for her mother. There were handmade greeting cards with dried flowers stuck on them looking pretty, despite being withered. She picked some.

His silent presence filled her with a sense of dread. With every passing minute, some inexplicable intimacy was growing too. The next shop had idols of Gods carved in stone and wood. They just went into while away the time. There were carved stony figures of Ganesha, Lakshmi, Saraswathi, Radha-Krishna and several others. She stared at the celestial embrace of Krishna and Radha with the flute in his hands and the pot of water spilt across their feet. It was made of sandalwood, had a delicate fragrance and the wistful expression on Radha's face was captured too.

"Whose love do you admire more? Radha or Meera?" He asked.

"Both were wives of other men. Having sixteen thousand wives was not enough, he enticed other men's wives too."

"Love is not politically correct. When even religion understands that why can't you?" Then did he understand Emma? She did not want to bring that up.

"Both loves were self-defeating. Radha loved Krishna, still went on to marry another man. Meera married to another man, loved Krishna all her life. I think he was only an ideal for her, she never walked out of her marriage."

"Is marriage the goal of every love? If not is it useless? Life itself is not eternal. Forever is lonely evenings by a television set and silent dinners with weather talk and sound of spoons.

Does this not look like love to you?" He pointed at the statue of Radhakrishna. It was only a moment creating an illusion of eternity.

The shop keeper a middle-aged man, astutely clever, approached Dhruva asking if he wanted to buy it. They murmured no and walked out of the shop. She turned to go back to the hotel. Dhruva said, "You are going back only in the night, you can come back to the beach in the evening if you want. I will be there." She smiled and left.

She entered the blue room, called the room service for lunch. Looking out of the French windows she ate her lunch and fell exhausted on the soft bed. She tried to think of Sagar but it was Dhruva's stare that came back to her. How could she connect with someone on so many planes in such a short time? He had blown away all those fears that inhabited this room just last night. Had he blown away the dreams too? The big fears seemed small but big dreams seemed smaller too. The light flowing from the windows pricked her eyes. She closed the curtains, lit one aromatic candle and looked at the melting wax. The margins of the candle melted, resembling a long trail with a single teardrop at the end. She fell asleep.

She woke up dreaming of Sagar with another woman, laughing and looking very hunky-dory. She felt sick and depressed like she always did after a deep nap in the afternoon. She would go back to Sagar tonight, she consoled herself.

That black hole in the heart which his absence created could not be filled by another man. Once the boundaries were broken, to redraw them with that person was sheer torture. First, the body had to be withdrawn, no more settling into each other's contours. Then meetings would have to be avoided. The telephone wouldn't ring with his voice. She would be picking it several times to hear the dial tone howl and ensure that the phone was in order. Then came those bouts of sobbing wrenching her heart out of its rib cage in the early morning hours, when the sky was empty with no moon or the Sun, just millions of lonely stars, shivering in the cold with their pride. No, she would never survive travelling that road again. This was the milestone; she would not take a single step alone hereafter.

Life had to be lived with one person. She could not handle tearing up some more photographs, avoiding songs and streets. Maybe she had not connected with Sagar on many planes but she had conjured up dreams.

He lived in all her tomorrows, waiting to happen. Lives waiting to be born out of their love. This was no childhood comrade from whom she could reclaim her scented eraser which was given by her the previous day when he was absolutely charming and today when he is horrid to be retrieved promptly. However lame it sounded, they shared history. She recalled his palms like paws clutching hers as he fell asleep in late-night movie shows sitting next to her. She removed his photograph from her purse and stared for long taking in all the features.

She wore a long black top with little mirrors twinkling, sewed on them. Sun drowned and street lights blinked on. She picked up her maroon bag from the cupboard and checked out of the room. This time the receptionist was warm, almost cordial. Anu had passed his test of chastity. She walked up to the beach.

There were many people now. Clusters of families and friends sitting around. The smell of food flavored the air. Human voices in a sort of unison like the screeching of birds of different breeds united by their collective feeling of homecoming in the evenings.

Where to find Dhruva in this swarm of people? Being alone amidst this crowd was scary. She quickly retraced her steps when Dhruva caught up with her.

"So you give up on me so easily?" She was relieved to see him. His eyes silently appreciated her silver earrings and her softer rounded look. They walked along the stretch of the beach towards a less crowded spot. Dhruva carried her baggage.

The waves appeared like silver-painted pleats of a black sari. The sky overhead was vast and unbroken unlike the sky of her city that was broken into pieces by tall buildings. The thin moon like a piece of nail clipped by a clipper or a cartoon smile followed them uninterrupted without playing hide and seek behind concrete structures. The grains of sand were pricking her feet, boldly finding their way into her sandals.

"So you are all set to go back and face the world?" "Not the world, just one person who may be going out of his mind searching for me." His expression was blank. There was silence. He seemed distracted. Someone was strumming a guitar somewhere, a lilting tune and a human voice full of emotion accompanying it, lyrics were muffled, could not be deciphered.

The ocean continued to move with all her waves dancing tirelessly, now appearing vain as she had a full floor of audience. The little girl who was selling puffed rice in the morning came back looking shy and neat in a green skirt and yellow blouse. She said her father was better and was frying fish in some corner of the beach.

Anu gave her ten rupees which she accepted gratefully and ran away. She looked at Dhruva again and cleared her throat. It was half-past eight, she had to go. Now he looked achingly vulnerable like a lost child.

"When I was younger I used to draw faces and when some features did not look like my imagination I used to erase. I was careful to use a pencil and draw lightly. But as I grew I was more confident of my talent to translate imagination to reality so sketched with a felt pen. Now, if ever I am dissatisfied, I can't erase it, it would tear the page, I have only one page." Dhruva nodded as though he understood. He touched her cheek softly and disappeared in the crowd.

She understood in a flash why Emma had stayed on with the doctor for a year. But she understood better what had caused her to go back to her past.

~***~

2. dissected language

~~~~~~~~~~~~~~~~~***~~~~~~~~~~~~~~~

"Language is alphabet in disorder." – Gertrude Stein

It was the smell of death; it was the smell of wanting to preserve death. Eleven aluminum tables stood in that hall each contained a cadaver. The cadavers were dead for a while; they were taken out of formalin tank. Rigor Mortis had gone on and they were all stiff, the skin was blackened. But when I did go near them, they appeared like real people who were dead. I tried not to close my nose. Though the cadavers may not be offended, it would appear inappropriate. Death must mean more than just the smell of flesh not allowed to rot.

I looked out of the large French windows of the hall. There were lush green trees, a bird on one of the branches, blue sky with white cotton clouds strewn around. It looked unreal like a postcard. Eleven dead bodies waiting to be dissected seemed more real than the silent life surrounding it. They were all naked, covered in transparent plastic sheets. The hall felt cold like a cemetery. I felt like a prop in a diorama, rendered lifeless by a taxidermist and every dead or living being was just a caricature, unreal.

I was uncomfortable with the nudity, especially around the two female bodies in the hall. I looked away from the pubic areas of the dead. I moved away from
~~~~~~~~~~~~~~~~~

them, avoiding eye contact with other students in the hall. Many of these bodies belonged to those not claimed by any living person.

To be dissected by medical students aspiring to learn human anatomy was not their agenda before death. I was clad in my brand new apron, fiddling with brand new dissection blades safely in a dark red velvet case. My brand new classmates were speaking in hushed voices; I lacked the confidence to whisper small talk. I preferred to have attended the funerals.

All the eleven cadavers were once living human beings, brushing their teeth, washing their hair, wearing their clothes, feeling ashamed if anyone saw their genitals. Yet, now they were here… bodies without a feeling.

When I had seen funeral processions of a dead body on the streets with a music band in tow, I was irritable, as if the dead man can appreciate this circus? Why can't they silently cremate the body? The pyramids of Egypt awaiting the resurrection of the mummies or a tomb-like Taj Mahal, a stony poem or an awesome obituary… were acts of love towards the dead. What if those left behind did not remember? I thought of the obituaries column with a sort of respect now, carrying the names of those left behind. There were no cries here, no lover feeling possessive of this nudity, no child attached to the last shirt on his father's body, smoothing the wrinkles.

I looked into the eyes of a guy, a classmate with huge eyes. One dead body between us on the table. He seemed affected by my presence, he was idly curious about the dead body. He feigned an academic interest by quickly looking at the Cunningham manual when our eyes met. I may have looked deeply sad as though I knew the dead person lying on the table.

A middle-aged man entered the hall. He beamed importantly, "Good day! Students. I am Doctor Prakash. I will supervise the anatomy practical of dissection of upper limbs and thorax. First of all, you must respect the human body; I will not tolerate anyone holding their nose. Respect is the keyword. A hundred students for eleven bodies, not a bad ratio. One cricket team for the entire nation… Ha Ha!" He was quite impressed by his own joke.

He seemed to have grown up in this hall, on this smell, he seemed to thrive on it. As an afterthought, he roared, "Respect!" Just that one word made him feel powerful. He started to call out register numbers dividing us into groups of ten, leading each group to one table. After calling out my register number he chuckled, "Bad luck!"

I frowned; luck had nothing to do with dissection. He did understand that I did not get his joke, he explained, "Female bodies have more adipose tissue, they stink more. " I felt myself blushing, as though he had alleged me of stinking. *Was this respect?'* The feminist consciousness of mine whimpered. I fiddled with the buttons of my apron as if some completely feminine body part of mine was a colossal waste and just adipose tissue. I thought of Simone De Beauvoir. She would not have been polite to Dr. Prakash's facts about the second sex.

The corpse on the table was that of a middle-aged woman. The coarse features suggested a hard life, the soles of her feet had cracked heels, and her nails had chipped polish. She had a metal ring around her finger, perhaps due to the Rigor Mortis they could not remove it. Was that a gift from some unfaithful lover?

Her breasts had a moderate size; there was a bruise on her shoulder. I tried to imagine a little mouth suckling and then growing up and leaving her. Maybe, she had no children. Would she have loved someone in her life? Her face was serene; she probably did not know that she was going to die... and die all alone. There were some flower designs tattooed on her forearms and a blue dot on her chin. She definitely had a family in childhood. I tried to imagine a child with her features.

The smell continued to nauseate me. I remembered reading that olfactory cortex in the brain was the ancient brain, alongside limbic cortex where all emotions did circuit. Photograph of my mother did not have her safe smell. Any man using my father's aftershave would get my instant trust. I was beginning to feel homesick or seasick on a ship with eleven cadavers.

There was a short boy with a thick bifocal lens in my group. "Hi! Guys, I am Vishesh from MES college. I had an aggregate of 99.99%, securing the first rank in the Common Entrance Test." He said all of it in one breath, expecting applause. I thought of the Olympics gold medal winner from Japan who was not told that her mother was dying of cancer so as to facilitate her concentration. He seemed to have suffered to get here, he sounded like a stoic. He did take the silence in his stride. "The first lesson will be the dissection of the hand, I have been told. I have read most of it. It has the largest representation in the cerebral cortex. I can start the dissection if you guys permit me."

A girl with an oily plait and some marks of blessings on her forehead from several powerful Gods raised her voice, "I had 100% in Biology which is the highest for the state. I have a brother in the final year. You are right, dissection of the hand is the first class; I am familiar with the instruments of dissection also. Are you?"

A tall boy stammered, "This body has to be shared by all of us. Just the two of you dissecting the hand is not how it is supposed to be. In anatomy practical and viva voce, we too will be examined for our knowledge." The race had begun with everyone wanting to cut up this woman, with her shriveled breasts, closed eyes and an outstretched hand with that unfaithful ring…

I shifted weight from my right leg to the left; I felt an ache in the arch of my feet. Perhaps my classmates were immortal angels, they flew over the issue of death, oblivious and blithe. The boy with huge eyes looked amused as the audience in a wrestling contest. He saw that I was stupefied. He stared at my hand placed on the backrest of a chair, plucking at the nylon threads. I withdrew my fingers into a fist.

"Come on, name the bones of the wrist, you need to know the skeleton." The girl challenged the short boy. Perhaps this was Eve asking Adam to count his ribs. The hearing was not adjourned. Though I hoped it would be.

I stared at my small wrist wearing a new watch from Titan with moon dial. The studious owl looked at her sullen. Now she seemed to be in charge. "There is a mnemonic — *She Looks Too Pretty Try to Catch her*', Scaphoid, Lunate, Triquetral, Pisiform, Trapezium,

Trapezoid, Capitate and Hamate. So easy! My brother taught me. "The group was a bit subdued.

I looked at the broken heart line on the palm of the dead woman, Cheiro's book of palmistry was familiar to me. I was still trying to predict if ever I will fall in love and have children. At the bottom of my little finger, on the mount of mercury, there were thin slanting lines and Cheiro called them "medical/healing stigmata." I was reassured that I could heal someone in pain. I wanted to predict the life ahead of me and this girl had actually sat and memorized the names of bones of the wrist. Suddenly I had a doubt, maybe Cheiro was wrong. Maybe, I was the wrong candidate for this course. I was not sure if I could skin this woman, layer by layer… like messing up with a doll, with which I was not interested playing.

That was when a tall fair girl in a long skirt and painted lips came in, accompanied by a clerk; she brought in a faint fragrance of perfume with her. Dr. Prakash spoke to her and she opened a book, it looked similar to the Bible, she read from the book, haltingly. Her eyes were unsure, though her stance was ready for a battle. She was a foreigner; she joined in the last group. Dr. Prakash removed all the instruments of dissection and brandished them like an experienced soldier with hunting knives, explaining the techniques. The oily plait was eager to show off her knowledge. I continued to stare at the crevices of the corpse, her half-opened mouth. She had a vaccination scar on her thigh; it was shaped like a kidney. So she definitely had a mother as a child, I felt a bit placated by that scar.

I wished to be told her name at least. Whom can I ask that? I pondered. The class was over, no dissection happened that day. As we moved out of the class, was the foreigner girl. I smiled at her. She seemed relieved, eagerly walked towards me with an outstretched hand.

"Hi, I am Asrin Ataei from Iran; I am from the capital of Tehran." Her English sounded like an exotic dialect. I asked her where she was put up, was she in the hostel? I was a day scholar. She apologized and opened the book that looked like a Bible again; she read it from the end, the right end of a line back to the left. It was a Persian - English dictionary. I liked the fact that their written world was in the opposite direction, so would it make English less or more confusing? So, nothing was universally a correct direction, I felt relaxed that there were no absolutes. She was a paying guest in a house close to mine. She had to pass the Test of English as a Foreign Language in one month, and then she could understand the lectures. I nodded.

I asked her casually if she liked the class. She shook her head sideways, "Nah, very bad, everyone talking about cutting." Perhaps because of the paucity of words, her expression was intense. She felt exactly like I did, I could tell that. I am not sure why, but my eyes felt moist. She noticed, she could have ignored it, like we often do in our civil society but she was upset and held my hands in hers, chanting "No! No!" quickly turning the pages of her dictionary searching for a word, she gave up frustrated. The dictionary could not translate her feelings.

She was slightly older than me, I could see. Or maybe it was her make-up. She said in a grave voice, "You, me, we are living… No?" I thought it was profound, yet it was precarious, and death was so completely final. I pressed her soft hands. I guess the friendship between two persons cannot be measured by the number of words exchanged or the amount of time they have known each other.

Our seniors wanted to rag us whatever that meant. I don't know what they did to the guys. Perhaps that word like the viral fever was non-specific. Sometimes it could get fulminating, vicious… almost a killer disease, or it could be as simple as a common cold. Our seniors looked studious, awkward they assumed a fake bravado when they looked at us, sizing up who is hot, the regular boy meets girl routine. Some girls bonded with each other when they were picked on by the guys, learning to flee in a flock or hiding in some corners of the college building together and playing silly games… like during a power cut, in the absence of light people feeling the other, touching to see if there is someone with a palpitating pulse.

I did not mind chatting with strangers asking me stupid questions like who is in your heart or proposing to some arbitrary guy who was too shy to even meet my gaze. Asrin was picked on the first day; they thought because of her attire, she was interesting. I was with her, I asked her not to display the holy dictionary and to say helplessly "Persian". Asrin quickly caught on to the game, most seniors heard "Persian" to every question. I cheered heartily. They finally nicknamed her as the Unidentified Perfumed Object (UPO) and had their last laugh.

I think it was when she was trying to write the time table carefully by drawing a square and struggling with the spellings of Anatomy, Hematology, and Physiology. I moved next to her and wrote it for her. She was effusive in her body language of gratitude. Somehow I was comfortable with her wordless articulation. We did become friends, she visited my family, stayed in our house and we did learn and mugged up the names of all the bones for Osteology tests.

The domestic help in our house discovered the skull and bones in my cupboard. Occasionally feared me as though I was a witch! I enjoyed scaring her saying that the skull did come alive on no moon day and told me about his life and we were friends!

Asrin was a quick learner and surprised me with her newly acquired vocabulary and honesty of expressions. She read out Omar Khayyam, translating it to English, making me cry. She would often say, 'You need a sternum to love! A huge sternum!' I would tell her how during the Second World War soldiers fell in love with refugees who did not know their language and married the girls. But after their wives learnt the language, divorces increased! She would laugh saying that she would never divorce me!

There was an impending war between Iraq and Iran at that time. Asrin had a younger brother who was only fourteen years old but would be forced to go to war if he remained in Iran. So, her parents decided to send him to India for studies so that when he attains sixteen years and be called to participate in the war he would be away.

In the same academic year, we were also expected to dissect the heart out of a live frog and record the beats on a revolving drum, with a pointer attached to the innervated heart. Kindness to animals was not yet a fashion or a law. So every medical student had to cut this three-chambered heart of the frog and record the heartbeats for physiology practical examinations. A jumping frog was pitched to a wooden board paralyzing his spinal cord. I found it gruesome.

The tall boy was clubbed with me. It was two monsters against this one hapless frog. I mused about the princess who kissed the frog and converted him in to a prince… sigh! Though I had no intentions of kissing the frog or transforming him magically. I certainly did not want that cute valentine card model three-chambered heart, one auricle and two ventricles dissected out of him. My classmates as always, were keen on mastering this technique. Open heart surgeries were being done on humans, why should this frog lose his heart? For Gods to learn their game?

I remained stubbornly reluctant, criticizing the boy who did it as he did not question the rules. I was observed to be inert and asked for an explanation by the head of the department who occasionally came to the labs. The professor had an inexpressive face, was definitely intimidating, and because he questioned me, he was given a lengthy explanation by me about the ethics of dissection and the lack of necessity here. I presumed he was impressed. He probably liked a young girl who could voice her conviction. He was used to machines that obeyed him and answered what was in the textbook faithfully like parrots. Suddenly, once in a few years there was a mind and here, it had a body! He noticed.

I liked the fact that he treated me as a human being and merely let it go. He did not argue with me, said that during exams I would have to lose marks, it was a risk I could take if I compensated by doing well in other hematology practical test of pricking my finger and examining the blood. He lacked the power to change the system. Was he apologizing for the system? My classmates thought I was getting away due to my audacity and I thought I was very smart. And I had saved a frog.

Asrin's brother did not resort to the dictionary, he often did brilliant dumb charades, irritating Asrin who wanted him to pass TOEFL quickly and join the school. He was mischievous; I often saw that he was a little boy who neither understood war, nor the value of his father's money that had procured his exit to India. Asrin retold her splendid mastery of English with my help and how inadequate her brother was. But it had no effect on Ali, he was a tall child. His only passion was a Bike. His father bought him a bike within two months of his arrival to India.

I had stayed away from riding a cycle as a child since I was squeezed in the wrong place by a cyclist before I even touched a cycle. Now, I watched Ali's fascination with the bike, the way he washed it… I asked Asrin if I could learn to ride from him, in exchange for teaching him English. She readily agreed, she also wanted to ride the bike. She owned a car, mostly came to college driving. But the car was just a mode of transport and the bike was something else.

I, Asrin and Ali started to ride the bike on Sunday afternoons; I fell down several times as I had no two-wheeler balance. And Ali not knowing English often would not know to shout instructions, he merely prevented collisions with silent trees and slip to dirty ditches. I had pressed the accelerator and not the brakes and occasionally half-climbed a tree. Ali was helplessly laughing at my plight, Asrin cursing him in Persian.

I did get the balance one fine day and the primordial joy of locomotion was felt in my gut, the pit of my stomach felt light and empty as I rode down the long road and wished it would never end. Like coming down a giant wheel, it was a childish sensation of pure bliss. I forgot English and any other language, as I felt like a movement, like the wind. I did finally understand why boys did not feel lonely when they were riding. How possible it was to love movement, how close to flying it was. I felt strangely independent of the earth beneath me.

Ali laughed that he had taught me to ride much before I taught him English, I felt a bit guilty as a teacher. I continued with renewed enthusiasm to teach English and Ali tried to concentrate, Asrin would translate my lessons. And often a quarrel would erupt between them.

Final exams of the first year began; I and Asrin were preoccupied with studying. She sometimes came to my house to study as she got nervous. I would study alongside, calming her. The day before the last exam of that term, we spent a long time talking in her car. She was extremely restless, I presumed it was due to the exam and tried all my tricks to get her to concentrate.

Biochemistry felt simpler to me than Anatomy, more abstract hence less intrusive. She left before the sunset. The next day, Asrin was absent for the examination. I finished writing the exam, wondering what could have possibly caused her to be absent. Those were the days of phone booth connecting places, a cordless worked for short distances. Mobile phones were not invented yet, we still had privacy. I called the landline of her landlady.

"Ali died in the bike accident last evening. The body is being autopsied. Asrin is with a few Iranian friends who are helping her with the legal formalities." It was like an announcement for fire outbreak or weather forecast for an earthquake, said in a calm collected voice, totally devoid of emotion like in a dream. I was not sure if I heard right or was my cochlea and the auditory nerve was interpreting the signals wrongly. The landlady was mostly absent, this was a domestic helper. She seemed to be saying this not for the first time. Perhaps she had a few hours and rehearsals to get used to this information. I wish I was condemned to amnesia or would wake up making it undone.

I wanted to be with her, wherever she was. So 'yesterday' it seemed like a million years ago when she was struggling to focus on Biochemistry, her brother was battling with death? He did not know "English" the link between Indians, the remnant of colonialism. How could they have informed her? It had to be a traumatic brain injury, I tried not to recall the mangled remains of injured animals I had sometimes seen on the highway. I had flashes of Ali beaming at me, standing under a tree when I first got the balance of a two-wheeler to my utter surprise. I should have taught him 'English'.

My eyes blurred with tears of guilt. And professor Rao, the physiology teacher who had listened to the argument of my human right for the frog with the three-chambered heart almost collided with me. He looked at my eyes, as usual, there was no pretense between us; for him, honesty was a virtue and not obedience. My eyes expressed just sheer agony. He noticed, "Can you come with me?"

I sat in front of him, trying to reconstruct yesterday with the minimum details I had gathered over the phone. He was a patient listener. In the government hospital attached to the college where I studied, an autopsy was being done. He knew the professor of Forensic Medicine, I could not truly hear his conversation over the phone, I heard him say,

"Yes. Ali Ataei…" "Yes, very young, less than 18." He looked at my blank, glazed eyes, "The body is in the autopsy room. They have finished, fracture of the skull, herniation of the brain stem, lacerated liver, long bone fractures of both femur and tibia. It would have been difficult to save this boy even in Breach Candy Hospital, even if father sold an oil well. Most probably your friend will be there, come I will take you to the Forensic lab."

I had nothing of so-called 'will' in my skull, I had no thoughts. I merely walked behind him like a mute animal finding it really difficult to breathe. I saw Asrin's friends and another older Iranian man, her guardian in the city standing there. They did come to me in a rush and in the typically Iranian accent English told me that Ali had met with an accident, a collision with a tempo traveller yesterday morning, and that he was wearing the helmet, yet his helmet was also shattered to pieces.

He was taken to another government hospital and they found Asrin's address from the notebooks in his backpack. He kept calling her name and had cried out 'Persian' hoping to find an interpreter. He was conscious for almost six hours and Asrin reached the hospital soon after leaving me, he died in her arms.

Professor Rao was standing next to me all the while, he ushered me into the Forensic Lab. I was still in the first-year Preclinical syllabus, because of Anatomy dissection of the cadavers I was desensitized to those cadavers in the hall; nothing had prepared me for the so-called body of Ali. He was naked on the aluminium table and the skin was cut up and stitched in the middle like a rucksack.

His face looked normal, fast asleep. It probably would take me a long time to watch a child sleep without fearing him not waking up. Professor spoke to the Forensic Medicine assistant professor about the injuries and asked for the quick dispatch of the body to the relatives. He looked at me thoughtfully and left. He did not make any sort of speech; the first few hours of grief had no language.

It is sort of impossible to explain the cruelty of life that includes death to someone younger, much younger. Knowing there is hope is essential when alive and somehow knowing there was little or no hope is essential when dealing with the dead body of a loved one. So, he had tried to console me with hopelessness, though I liked him less for that. Even though it was hurting I still wanted to believe there was a place somewhere he could be revived.

Life imitated death in morbid stony silence. I spoke to Asrin over the phone surrounded by her Iranian friends who were weeping. She was calm; she wanted me to come to her guardian's house where she was going to stay for the day. Next morning, she was flying to Iran with the dead body of her brother to be buried in his country. When she heard that I was there in the Forensic Lab, her question was, "You did not see him without his clothes. Did you?" I managed to lie "No". She believed me.

That ultra-nakedness, absolute ghastly nakedness of a corpse that we both despised. His presence could not be stripped of its life… never in her mind. I was not given a choice to make informed consent, like cattle to the slaughterhouse.

That evening she was in her guardian's house, they urged her to eat, her parents called once in two hours. She kept on talking about how it could have been for him in the emergency room of the government hospital where we knew even anesthetics were in short supply. Knowing the language could have reduced the sense of alienation he felt in those hours of pain. His broken watch showed the time of the accident as 11:45 AM. She stared at it as we both tried to make the time go by, move on its own, without trying too hard to get through it by ourselves.

We tried to speak of things that could distance us from post mortem. I helped her pack his belongings in suitcases. One notebook where I had written English sentences that he had translated to Persian, Asrin picked up. The last sentence was how to say, 'I am in pain', 'I have a fever or I am sick'? I had not given the English version, I could not really remember why. She just said, "You keep it." It was too soon to accept death, and distribute his belongings as if he had written a will. He was riding to go to English classes. She had learnt it with me, he had not, and she did not want that book. I could not get the image of the autopsy out of my mind. We silently packed his clothes; a piggy bank with few rupees he had saved upon her insistence.

It was a hazy night. I remember her face in the airport clad in black. When our eyes met, I recalled her way of consoling me the first day of dissection, now it was not enough, we sort of lost each other in that airport of complete goodbyes. It was not a choice; a total numbness pervaded many layers. Since I had to walk, talk and function on the upper ground and not whimper at the bottom of a well. Presuming that love can survive muteness…. One quick hug and she disappeared.

As I travelled back in a taxi home, I saw a young man on a bike, having that immeasurable joy of movement. That sense of being the wind did not need words. I realized joy had no language, it had a smile.

~***~

3. night jasmines

~~~~~~~~~~~~~~~~***~~~~~~~~~~~~~~

It was a chilly morning in late October. Nights grew longer and colder with each passing day, observed Vasundhara. A vessel of milk to which a spoon of curd was added the night before had failed to ferment. She added another spoon of curd to it and placed it behind her old Godrej refrigerator as a heat source to curdle it.

She lifted the grinding stone, under it was a muslin clothed small sac. She touched its surface for sprouts. She had put in it green gram dhal soaked in water to sprout. There was no germination. She carried the small sac to a corner in her garden where it would receive sufficient warmth. Life needed Warmth she mused wryly.

As a whiff of cold air rustled her sari pleats, she hugged herself. She had germinated with no warmth as if to push away this stray thought, she tied all her grey hair into a neat knot. She boiled water for making the coffee decoction, her lonely emotions stirred again. It is this weather she grumbled, misty mornings beckoned old fractures to hurt again and loneliness like a disease gnawed her insides. That was when her husband Professor Chandramouli walked in, to announce that he would not be going to work that day.
~~~~~~~~~~~~~~~~

"What is happening to him?" Vasundhara thought to adjust her spectacles and staring hard at her husband. He was taking leave from work for the third time in the week.

Professor Chandramouli was in his early sixties. He had served as an atomic physicist in the National Institute of Atomic Physics all his life. Institute had acknowledged his innumerable invaluable contributions to the field and had bestowed the honorary professor's post to him. In order to facilitate research and academic activities, he was given the keys to the main Laboratory and the hall containing mainframe computers. He often claimed that if he were to breathe clean air devoid of scientific gases his health would deteriorate! Such a man was so indifferent to his work off late, Vasundhara was stunned.

Last week he absented from work alleging that someone had stolen his lab keys. After rummaging the entire house, finally found it where he always kept them, in his bookshelf.

He would often ridicule her as Vasundhara S.S.L.C who could count only the number of cashews in Pongal and nothing else.

But yesterday he had handed over the Bank passbook to her, and asked her to manage his finances!

Vasundhara had agreed in confusion and dismay. Should she take him to a doctor? This thought was buzzing in her head like a bee that would neither keep quiet nor go away. Her tired eyes wandered towards the daily newspapers on the table. They were untouched. Yes! Several months had passed since he read them with interest.

Earlier when he was reading the papers, she was not supposed to breathe a word. Not just while reading papers, he had never really asked her to speak, ever. To him I am just a machine to churn coffee and manufacture edible food, she sighed. And of course, a womb to house his babies. After two daughters when she delivered a son, her husband was elated. He had asked her magnanimously if the name 'Aprameya' was alright, she had haltingly replied with fear it would be better to name him Ajith as Aprameya sounded ancient.

"So the eminent scholar with the qualification of S.S.L.C tutors me about modernity." He had joked, words dipped in sarcasm. Her eyes felt moist. Later when their son passed the prestigious I.A.S examinations and was posted to Pune, Professor had evinced no paternal pride nor blessed him. "To serve politicians who have not even passed the third standard, why to pass these silly exams," he had commented.

She saw her six-foot one-inch tall son stoop his shoulders, and wipe his brow of sweat, drooping corners of his mouth, controlled disappointment etched in all his features. She clenched her fists as if she could hold her son's dreams tightly in them and prevent them from being dashed to the ground. He was so much like her always wanting approval from his father. Their love for each other was never enough, either for her or for him. She longed for her husband and he for his father, instinctively sympathizing with each other as they groped in the darkness of Professor's devotion to science.

When their daughter Maheshwari aspired to study in America even before marriage, Vasundhara had protested going on an indefinite hunger strike. Vasundhara knew in her maternal heart that Maheshwari with all her new-fangled ideas of feminism was most susceptible to male attention. The way she danced to her father's theorems and atoms or whatever attention he gave, her pursuit of science just proved that.

But her husband refused to yield and bought her tickets to Sabarmati Ashram and asked her to continue fasting there and not die under his roof. When Maheshwari won the prestigious 'BEST YOUNG SCIENTIST' award he was so proud of his decision to have sent her abroad. Then she visited India with a white man called Max calling him her husband. Marriage was just a contract even in India, she said. Max was not even a scientist. She noticed her husband was also awkward dealing with this strange creature with yellow long hair. Now, she was divorced. This is also just a paper I suppose, thought Vasundhara. They talk as though it is respectable to divorce in a foreign country.

Malavika, her younger daughter completed her degree and married the groom chosen by her parents. But she gave birth to a mentally challenged child. Her father never once carried that child - his only grandchild. Her husband's sister also had a retarded child, she was sure they were the genes from his side of the family. But her daughter would flinch each time someone noticed the retardation of the child as though it was her fault alone. Genes they say, whoever wants to pass on defects to their progeny, and intentions don't matter at all, is it?

Malavika stopped coming home though she was in the same town. Vasundhara wiped her tears. Why was she revising and reviewing all his faults now and hurting herself? Nothing was new. Her skin was silent and dense after years of pain.

Something was new. This morning when she was doing her puja Chandramouli came to her and asked her to sing Sri Chakra Rajasimhasaneshwari, a *kirtana* saying that she sang it so melodiously and he longed to hear it! She was completely taken aback, as far as she knew, he regarded music as a weakness, and never listened to her singing. Had he actually listened to her and enjoyed it? Foolishly, Vasundhara was shy and joyous like a new bride. Unwilling to relish this unexpected compliment she was reviewing a lifetime of neglect and insults.

She heard a bell ringing, no it was not in her imagination, it was the phone. She expected her husband to receive it. He ignored it. Well, this was another novel act. Earlier he would talk over the phone for hours, but lately he seldom received phone calls and refused to answer those who did call him. He was not reading his books. The dustbin in his room was filled with sheets of paper where few words were written, often spelt wrongly and were struck off.

She had come across waste papers earlier also in his room, but something was different; she could not put her finger on it. The writing on these pages was childish, some alphabets scattered on white pages, and there were no words. Maybe she should ask him to get his eyes checked by a doctor. Couldn't he see properly or was it something else? He was not sleeping in the nights; he would be walking all around the house, up and down the stairs, searching for some unknown memento it seemed.

When she had first discovered her husband to be absent in their bed and someone was moving around the house at night, Vasundhara was so petrified that she chanted *Vishnu Sahasra Nama* tightly closing her eyes. Now she was used to his nightly prowls.

This was like doing mental arithmetic when she added two numbers, third one slipped her mind. She remembered teaching Malavika additions with fingers and toes. That child had removed her shoes and socks in the classroom as she could not count without seeing her toes! This memory brought her a smile. She decided to make some coffee for her husband and searched for him. She found him standing outside the washroom, half bent, peering inside.

Across the hall, she questioned, "What are you looking at?" He turned and looking at her, as though he had found a rescue boat in a stormy sea, his eyes streaming with tears and arms automatically outstretched he ran towards her, hugging her, he wept.

Between sobs, he said, "I could not find the kitchen, I could not find you, I am lost Vasu, I am lost!" Vasundhara had never found her husband thus. Over the years she had come to rely on his indifference as his strength and her own silent unresisting stoic reaction as her strength. She had forgotten how to care for a husband. She was a mother by instinct. Some walls crumbled within her, she consoled him saying she was there all along at home, maybe they should visit an eye specialist, and maybe he was just tired. She made him sit on the sofa in the hall.

Since the coffee was spilt all over her sari, she had to change. She spoke to him loudly and clearly as though addressing a child, said she will be back in a minute and went in. She opened her old almirah, looked at her modest collection of saris smelling of naphthalene balls. She absently looked at her nine-yard pink coloured wedding sari. There were no pressed dried flowers whispering past romantic moments of her life. Just one blackened lotus under yellowed newspaper lining her saris. It was given to her by the *pujari* before Aprameya's birth. She hardened her sinking heart against her husband, wore a purple sari like armor and stepped out.

She heard loud voices engaged in an argument. One of them was her husband's. She rushed out. Postman of their area Peter Snell was standing out. Recently Chandramouli had started to use electronic mail for all his correspondences and ridiculed Peter Snell as the agent of Snail mail befitting his name. He called him Peter the Snail. Peter humored the Professor, laughing at himself. Vasundhara liked the affable young man.

Today there was a mail for Aprameya and her husband protested that there was no one by that name in their house and their son was Ajith. Chandramouli behaved as though Peter was a stranger. Vasundhara was confused; remembering her songs, identifying their son by the name Ajith (which was her suggestion many years ago). Was he trying to impress her? He had never tried to please her even when they were newly married so why now?

Peter was too stunned to speak. When Professor saw Vasundhara, he abruptly stopped the argument, like a puppy acknowledging the authority of a master, quietly and obediently went inside.

Peter stood beside Vasundhara and said in a low, hushed tone, "What has happened to Sir, Madam? He did not recognize me at all. He does not even recall the name of his son. Have you shown him to a doctor? He has not shaved the left side of his face, he has not put his left arm in the sleeve of his shirt… there is something definitely wrong. Please call your son, Madam. Take Sir to a doctor, don't let him go out alone, he may lose his way."

Peter had the objectivity of an outsider which Vasundhara lacked having lived in professor's shadow all her life. Her mouth felt dry, she felt faint. She stumbled her way to the phone, dialed her son's number.

(2)

I was working as a psychiatrist in an institute dedicated to the care of the mentally ill. I was posted as the duty doctor, so had to work from eight in the morning to the next morning till eight in the casualty. It was evening. I was sipping a cup of coffee and looking at the evening sky, purple and pink colors splashed across it. It was beginning to get dark, slowly. All natural processes were so slow and subtle, I thought. It does not become dark in a moment nor does it become a day in a moment.

Slowly but steadily it changes. There was a bush of night jasmines below the window. As it was blooming, its strong fragrance tickled my nose. I could not smell my coffee; it was as though I was drinking night jasmines. I was irritated with this untimely blooming like the delayed milestones of a baby. All birds were flying back to their nests, life on earth was aching to rest and these jasmines want to bloom now, why? Perverted flowers, I grumbled.

That was when the door opened, and an old woman with symmetric features and a young man who resembled her so much that it was obvious he was her son came in. Good looks don't metamorphose into bad looks with ageing I realized. A beautiful young woman becomes a beautiful old woman. "Patient is sedated doctor," said the nurse. I wanted the history and description of his complaints. Vasundhara volunteered. She described all the changes she had noticed in her husband, the son was not aware of them as he lived away in Pune.. After listening to her description of complaints I suspected that Professor was suffering from

Alzheimer's Dementia. I had to examine the patient to confirm my diagnosis.

In spoken language, names and words are forgotten and so language was sounding empty. At first, the patient responds to the clues/prompts provided by others. But as the disease progressed he could not. As he forgot the meaning of words he lost interest in reading. Many patients can read until the middle stages of the disease but can't understand the meaning of what they read. This might explain Professor's lack of interest in reading newspapers.

Calculations are upset from the start, as all mathematical applications require recent memory, this may be the reason why Professor handed over the Bank passbook to Vasundhara. Ability to remember the geography of familiar places is impaired. The patient gets lost in familiar places, lose their way while driving and may eventually become disoriented in their own homes. Professor seemed to have all these symptoms. Loss of this visuospatial skills manifests itself as dressing disturbance. Chandramouli had not worn the left sleeve, had not shaven the left face.

Memory is the spine of intelligence, it is the basis of all human relationships, including that sacred tie which a human being shares with himself. Hence personality alters too. Soft-spoken, gentle souls become short-tempered. Some others, arrogant all their lives become diffident and obedient like Professor. In this degenerative disorder of the brain, neuronal cells die. Reasons for this disorder are unknown. Heredity definitely plays a pivotal role. In these families, mental retardation is also common. Rate of the progress of the disease can be slowed with drugs, but the disease can't be cured. And memories which are lost can never be retrieved.

Professor Chandramouli woke up from his drugged sleep. I interviewed him at length and confirmed my diagnosis. I had to determine the stage of the disease, rule out the existence of other diseases presenting with similar symptoms. A battery of tests had to be run, and I had to educate his wife about the nature of the illness and strategies to care for him. So I asked for his admission to the hospital.

The next day I was asking him simple questions to assess the residual memory. His disease was past middle stages, so he could not even recall the arbitrary group of numbers let alone perform any arithmetic applications. He could not draw or even copy a cube. Tears glistened in his eyes and he was aware of his disability, so I stopped several times. I did not want to unnerve him and make him lose his confidence completely. Vasundhara stood near the door, murmuring words of consolation.

Professor did not remember his daughter Maheshwari. He remembered his granddaughter Akhila, he called her very intelligent - this was untrue as the child was mentally challenged. My medical eyes perceived it as confabulation. But Vasundhara interpreted it as a hidden hitherto unexpressed affection for his grandchild. He strangely remembered his wife's name and several daily activities of hers.

I prescribed some drugs to improve his mood and sleep. I gave Vasundhara a simple book on Dementia. I taught her some methods to handle him without creating pressure on his remaining memory. After a detailed explanation by me about his disease and its inexorable course, Vasundhara and her son became despondent. The son irritable and impatient said, "Then you are only delaying death, is it not?"

I could understand his anger, however much he may have resented his father's arrogance and superior demeanor, he could not bear to see that proud man as a helpless blithering vegetable. Professor had identified himself completely with his intellect and today was forced to live without it. I spoke gently, "Man has not conquered death as yet. Some diseases have been conquered that is all. Man is still not immortal. All medicines only postpone death.

If you are pained to see your father, a brilliant scientist reduced to a retarded existence, I am sorry too. But the heart and brain cells once dead cannot be regenerated. All other organs in the human body can regenerate. Science is making efforts to grow them from stem cells and graft, to prevent the next generation from inheriting by applying gene therapy etc... but permanent treatment for this disease is still in experimental stages.

Once upon a time, there were no cures for Tuberculosis, Leprosy, and Plague. Today we have conquered all infective diseases. There might be dawn when we can cure Dementias. But today we can only slow the progress of this disease and ensure that the remainder of his life is peaceful."

As I was leaving the room Vasundhara came to me and said haltingly, "I have lived with him for the past forty long years. But he has changed now. He recalls my songs but has forgotten his science. He remembers me and all the petty details of my life. He recalls even my likes and dislikes. He recalls the name by which I wanted to call our son; he has forgotten what he named him. Our granddaughter whom I adore though she is retarded he thinks she is intelligent. Does it mean he loved me all his life and I simply did not realize or is it all part of the disease too? I thought my life was completely futile," she sobbed.

I was overwhelmed by this naked vulnerability. I did not dare to answer this question. Temporal lobes of the brain where the memory of sounds and tunes are stored remain preserved until the late stages of the disease. That may explain Professor remembering her songs. But this answer was for academically inclined doctors, and not for this woman longing for love.

What is love? It is all about remembering a series of moments shared with that person, is it not? Especially when they have reached that stage where looking back is where you find all your reasons to live on. Was she all that Professor remembered from his life? So indeed he loved her. Love was also a dependence. The rest of his life depended on her nurturance. Love which begins as an attraction in youth transforms into a comforting mutual dependence in old age, I suppose.

What caused these profound changes in him? Is it that as the sharpness of his intellect blunted, hitherto unexpressed human emotions were finding expression? Was it just self-interest? Or was it all due to disease? Did it matter what were the reasons? As long as it appeared to be love to Vasundhara it was enough was it not? I was holding her hand, waiting for her to stop crying. She did finally regain her composure. Amidst wrinkles on her face, I saw a small smile taking shape. In those eyes dimmed by hurts, I saw a gleam of newfound love.

Did it matter she found her love now? Yes, it was late, but nevertheless, she found it. Life seemed to be full of meaning now. Why shouldn't stars twinkle in a moonless dark sky? Why shouldn't jasmines bloom at twilight? Here they did.

4. at the end of a wave

~~~~~~~~~~~~~~~~~~~***~~~~~~~~~~~~~~~~

Shanthala slowly rocked the cradle, with a long thread tied to it. As she looked out she saw the tear-stained face of her third daughter, hesitantly standing at the threshold of her bedroom.

Shanthala called softly, "What is it, my little princess? Why are you crying?" There was a flurry of soft feet rushing to her bedside with a sob. Meenu's hair was a messy knot, hands were sticky, and she sobbed into her mother's lap. The stammer following uncontrollable sobbing in children ensued and Shanthala could decipher that it was all about the broken neck of her second daughter's doll. Meenu showed the red welt on her plump three years old arms, punished for that offence.

Where was Mariyamma, why had she left the children to themselves? Shanthala murmured some sweet nothings into her daughter's little ears which were red like the petals of a flower. Meenu turned and looked at the four days old baby in the cradle, "Can I give him five-star chocolate? A tiny piece will be enough for him I think." Shanthala wearily tried to remove the knots in her daughter's hair with her fingers; they were tremulous after the prolonged labor pain which she had endured.

"He has no teeth he can't eat chocolates now, he will choke if you put it into his mouth, don't you dare!"
~~~~~~~~~~~~~~~~~~~

Madhu stood like a glaring professor. She held the head of Rita in one hand and the body in the other. Shanthala tried to reason with Madhu, "She may have broken that by mistake, ask the Gorkha he will be able to fix it." Madhu was commanding, "I don't think you should trouble mummy, she has lost a lot of blood, doctor aunty said, so now come out."

Shanthala smiled weakly, Madhu reminded her of grandmother. Her grandmother who scolded her when she played in the sun "Now you will become so dark that no boy will want to marry you!" Then when she bathed her in the hot sweaty Mangalore climate Shanthala would admire the fat white smooth thighs of her grandmother, revealed because of the sari being tucked up her waist, she would put her little palms against her thighs to compare how dark she was.

Ajji (grandmother) was happy at her wedding, "The boy is fair, so my great-grandchildren may not be so dark after all."

He was happy that she bore him a son after three daughters. It proved his virility. When he had photographed the newborn baby without his nappy (asking her to remove the nappy) she was repulsed. Earlier whenever he played with little boys she had felt a stab of inadequacy, as though it was her defect that she gave birth to only daughters. She had fasted for sixteen

Mondays and dragged her little daughters to the Shiva temple. All the four pairs of hands folded in front of the lord pleading for a male child. Then on the sixteenth Monday, she had lit the entire temple with small lamps of *til* (sesame) seeds tied in little black clothes, soaked in oil.

Madhu stayed up with her most of that night tying up the little sacs, though she was only seven years old. She had asked Shanthala, "Ma, why is a boy better than a girl?" Shanthala thought for a while and said, "Because girls marry, become a part of another family and go away but boys stay with the parents."

"What if girls don't marry?"
"Then they become a burden on the family." came the quick reply. "Oh now I understand, whether she marries or not she is inferior to a boy." Madhu simply accepted that as a fact.

Shanthala had recovered her senses, "Because we have three daughters, I want a son, not because a boy is better." Somehow, Madhu was not convinced.

Jagannath was absent from the minute she had come back from the hospital. He was so eager to marry the moment he had seen her. But after the marriage ceremony was completed, he seemed to not seek her at all. Between long tours she was a pleasant interlude, the clashing of flesh, a rough brush of the skin, drenching by the fall of the rain inside, a sharp movement between a gasp and a sob, transforming into one animal with eight limbs like an octopus, stuck to one another by his gum. Then the slow sorting out of his hands disentangling from hers, her legs entwining his for hours, then she would faint discovering she was pregnant once again.

She would want him out of the house, like a hibernating moth she overslept, overate, with the unbearable heat of the pulsating life within her. He stayed away not partaking in the pride of her pregnancy. She would resolve that she would not wait for him; she wanted to keep him on hold withdrawing her soft flesh, make him suffer from that unreciprocated longing. With the advanced state of her pregnancy, even though it was her choice, it seemed like vulnerable enforced celibacy. Not at all an autonomous, empowered statement. She had seen this in him, he was attracted to what he could not possess, when someone or something completely belonged to him, he lost interest. It was always the thrill of the eternal chase, the allure of the "other".

Millions of sperms chasing that one ovum, when the external mating game was over the internal chase would begin. As she surrendered to that wave of passion, her contours cupped by his unyielding hardness, and her soul was washed in the waters of that ocean, there was fertilization, tadpoles picked up by the flowery tubes, breaking that shell of the ovum and a turbid rainbow form, shapeless mass growing in to a perfect human form, a microcosm within macrocosm.

Then, the pervasive fear of injuring the life within her, watching every step, the girlish careless springy stride replaced by the cautious slow movements of a tender shoot. The endless swim of the embryo, the little kicks waking her up in the nights. Growth was a dark process, like all creative processes, belonged to the night. How long does a seed stay inside the dark mother earth, before it finally shoots up shyly to see the sun? Like the suppressed screams of a virgin, screams of the new mother were also muffled.

When all that could be torn was torn, sheets and sheets of blood, amniotic fluid, were oozing out of her, in that divine moment when birth and death embraced each other, consciousness was clouded, and she would hear the cry of the baby. And the bitter disappointment when the doctor announced, "Look at your daughter! She is so lovely." So this time when she heard the word "son", her eyelids were forcibly, atrociously uplifted and she actually looked.

The family astrologer was summoned who was jubilant at the thought of receiving a hefty sum for his astounding predictions, the same man had predicted the same son twice before! Now that the baby was out of her womb, she felt like a deflated balloon with the rubbery folds of skin hanging around her waist, silvery streaks of cellulite over her abdomen and thighs. The conjunctiva was pale and the under eyes dark, that infinite exhaustion of the muscles which had pushed and pushed the baby out of her body. With the fullness of milk within her, soreness of the skin, engorged veins, she was oblivious to the world around her.

Jagannath was elated with the birth of the son, feeling proud as though he had done it. She recalled when her third daughter was born neither Jagannath nor anyone of his family had visited her. Her ageing father would carry the flask of hot coffee to her in the hospital, and to her cringing questioning look would reassure falsely, "Jagannath has a high fever, poor man how can he come?" Both were aware of the lie but he would lie anyway and she would pretend to believe it anyway. Fortunately, her little daughter did not have to pretend that she was wanted anyway. So she just cried and cried till her shrivelled up umbilical cord fell on her grandfather's lap. He was also a father after all.

Mariyamma came in heaving a sigh of relief. "I was searching them all around the house, here they are. I was preparing your mother's special *rasam*."

Shanthala was a little pacified. That special soup of black pepper was being prepared for her under the instructions of her mother, Mariyamma was not gossiping with the neighbours. Mariyamma was the chief editor of that road's special news bulletin, knowing important details such as the houses in which the men cooked, which woman wore a sleeveless blouse, which child will grow up to be a slut, and most importantly which of her neighbor bitched about her the most. So Mariyamma made her belong to that street and without her Shanthala would feel disconnected from her immediate surroundings like watching a movie without the sounds. Mariyamma was the soundtrack.

As the children left, Shanthala enquired about Jagannath obliquely, trying not to sound too eager as Mariyamma was quick to pick up wifely insecurities. She replied, "They were speaking about shuffling portfolios, too many phone calls, meetings." Shanthala coped with Industrial power gracefully. Being a dignified hostess to several distinguished guests, planning dinners and lunches in accordance with his tastes. She had forgotten what her tastes were, from food to sex, it was always Jagannath likes thick dosas, Jagannath likes butter for dosa and ghee for *holige* (a sweet chapatti made of jaggery and coconut). He does not like too much yellow dhal in *kosumbri* (a salad made of cucumber). He won't touch a dish made in ladies finger unless it is dry fried.

How did she like the food she ate no one ever asked her. When her mother reminded her that she liked coffee and not tea, she felt a quick tightening of her throat a hard lump. When she made chapattis, nicest ones with the best shape and color were for Jagannath, moderately good ones for the children, the burnt ones were for her and the servant.

She felt like a real person only with the children. "Mandakini, don't stoop your back, don't forget your kerchief; Madhu, don't talk too much; Meenu don't cry for everything like Pandribai (a local actress famous for tragic roles)." So that was one platform where she was omnipotent. The morning rush of packing their lunch boxes, coaxing them to eat, plaiting their hair, she was efficient. Once they were gone she would care for the house and herself in that order. The house was like a living organism, demanding to be groomed, constantly growing with its paraphernalia of smaller sized skirts and cycles, bigger sized books and shelves.

This was not a permanent fixture, she had moved houses so many times, the Baygon (insecticide) spraying of the new house, over boiling of milk, allocating clothes to various cupboards, she wanted a permanent home. She watched her little girls take out the cushions of the sofa and build a house between the handles of the sofa. One cushion was the roof another the wall, and they would make their small bodies smaller, wedging themselves into that narrow space. A torch would be taken with great delight to light up the house. Small toy plates would serve food for the guests! They never got tired of this silly game, Shanthala was tired of it.

Her little son was awake, crying for milk. As she nursed the baby she saw his huge eyes and lashes like caterpillars, they were so thick. She had milk flavoured with saffron, and carrot juice every day this pregnancy, and felt such pure joy at this small being's perfect lashes. They did tickle her breasts, it was the pleasure of an animal suckling the baby. Feeding was such an instinct of the mother for years; she attributed every tantrum, every bout of frustrated torrential tears to hunger. She would unwittingly rush with a plate of food when children cried.

She started to hum a lullaby, it was her son! She had a son at last! She saw a book of Bhagavad-Gita by the bedside. What was this doing here? It should have been in the *puja* room. She reached out for the book, the tear twitched with the stretch. When she opened the pages she saw a peacock feather, next to it a small pink feather. So this was Madhu's handwork. She was the collector of feathers, seashells, mica pieces, sandpaper, smooth pebbles, silver foils etc. Madhu peeped in, she was shy to see her mother feeding the baby. Shanthala laughed, "Come in, did you keep the Gita here, why?"

Madhu had the look of relief, "You told me once that, it was said in Gita that we should do our best and not bother about the result so I was scared what if it became a sister, so I kept this here just in case such a thing happened." Shanthala dropped her eyes.

"They told me that peacock feather will also give birth to a small feather, it never did that, I got so fed up waiting so I made it adopt this one." Shanthala smiled at this childishness. How can a dead feather give birth to another? But feathers which flew passively in the wind of the electric fan had a life of their own. They were the only symbols of wings, Madhu could hold.

She looked at Madhu's dried up elbows and called her to her side. As she applied Johnson baby cream to her elbows, Madhu looked at the baby on her mom's lap. He yawned, as he was satiated.

"Can I hold him?" Shanthala shifted that small human form wrapped in woollen and clothes on to Madhu's eager bony lap. He let out a small muffled cry. Then he did the unthinkable, he wet her skirt. Now she let out a big cry and startled the baby.

"I think he hates me, how could he do this?" Shanthala picked the little one and started to change his clothes. Mariyamma came in, "This means your brother loves you the most. Wait when he grows up whenever he is scared he will come running to you."

"So that he can do this nasty stuff? Thank you! I don't want." Madhu sulked. Shanthala reaffirmed Mariyamma's words; she knew that Madhu did not accept Mariyamma's words that easily. Mandakini was a stubborn child, willful, haughty, Madhu was easy to handle cooperative and warm, but she was inquisitive and asked uncomfortable questions.

She had asked Shanthala quite seriously why the three sisters should sleep in one room and Jagannath and she slept in the other? Shanthala said innocently, "I am scared to sleep alone." Madhu thought for a minute, "So am I, maybe it is better we sleep next to each other?" Shanthala had kissed her in a rush of maternal warmth.

Madhu mothered Meenu and so the sleeping arrangement remained unaltered. Shanthala would hear Madhu spinning bedtime stories, Meenu interrupting occasionally and Mandakini also listening quietly. The stories were of love, wars, famine, gods, faraway lands, unfelt profound sorrows and pathos. Shanthala would eavesdrop at times. On those nights, sounds were too loud and Jagannath was too late.

The doorbell rang, and she could hear the gleeful laughter of Meenu. She had not spoken much to Jagannath after the baby's birth, it was as though they were the common lucky survivors of a natural calamity. Both being in a tempestuous sea and were washed off to the calm shores, she was preoccupied rejoicing that she was alive. Now she had to look at the face of the co survivor.

When she had Mandakini barely a year and a half after her marriage, she was angry with Jagannath, ambivalent about the live doll at her breast. But there was so much of hunger in his touch; she was possessive of even his glance. When his eyes acknowledged a beautiful woman other than herself she would burn with jealousy. She was madly in love with his body, guarding it with her own, the signature of his love bites on her flesh.

Slowly physical passion ebbed, replaced by a maternal concern which Jagannath hated. Men could not lust after a mother or was it his flaw?

Jagannath entered the room and ascertained that the room was presentable. "Come in Priya, no formalities, you can come in." A young woman in her twenties, dressed in a modern outfit of a tight skirt and black blouse accompanied him. "Congratulations! Madam," she smiled. The face was nervous, eager for some approval.

On closer look, Shanthala thought the girl was pretty, in a highly anglicized way. The aquiline nose, high cheekbones, honey brown eyes, exceedingly fair complexion, a lot like Rita - Madhu's doll. The girl was not well endowed, kind of skinny but for the butt. This was like one female animal appraising the other in a contest. The tension was palpable, till Mariyamma arrived fussing over Jagannath. He appeared besotted with this girl, making her feel comfortable asking what she would like to drink. Priya in a faint irritable tone said, "Jagannath, you should at least introduce me to your wife". Shanthala strained to hear. "Priya is a journalist." Did she imagine the intimacy in their eyes when they looked at each other? She felt fat, clumsy, dark, and like an outsider. He was her husband, she was torn giving birth to his son, four days ago, but this young woman with firm supple body and ironed clothes was in command.

As though she read the stricken look on Shanthala's face, Priya spoke, "He was so elated about his son, he insisted that I should see the little darling, so is he asleep, can I see him?" Meenu who was sitting in quiet awe of this grown-up Rita, Goddess of Athens, simply got up and left the room. Madhu announced sternly, "If you can see the baby is asleep". Shanthala saw that Madhu was partially covered by the curtains but her voice was loud and clear.

Jagannath said angrily, "You should come in and address aunty respectfully!" Madhu came in and sat, with that grumpy "I don't really care" look which Jagannath abhorred.

Once in a quarrel between Mandakini and Madhu, Jagannath had wrongly judged Madhu to be guilty and she had walked away from home in a thin petticoat on one winter night. After that Jagannath was careful while dealing with her.

"You have such beautiful eyes!" exclaimed Priya looking at Madhu. But Madhu was not charmed "My little brother has better eyes and much better lashes," she could be clinically objective. Mandakini appeared with a tray of tea and biscuits, suitably humble and deferential towards the modern young woman. "You seem to have a whole team of cheerleaders," Priya remarked, tinged with sarcasm or was it betrayal? Jagannath smiled shyly and foolishly. He threw a glance at Madhu which made her wish to be unborn.

Shanthala politely asked, "So what are your future ambitions?" Priya serenely answered, "My father died when I was twelve years old, my mother is a nurse she reared me and my brother as a single parent. From the age of twenty, I am working and studying to acquire a degree." The girl looked vulnerable, sad, almost like a victim. Almost a poor waif. Maybe, she was searching for father figures? Shanthala was willing to approve of her. Jagannath smiled that ravishing college boy smile, "She writes exceedingly well. One of her recent write-ups in a leading daily caused a furore in the industrial circles."

He probably would have praised even a wart on her nose; if she did stink of sweat he may have said that it was fragrant like Gucci scent. Priya was embarrassed, Shanthala almost blushed but Jagannath continued his eulogy. Madhu fidgeted sensing some impropriety. "Why did your father die?" Now she had embarrassed even Jagannath. A shocked silence. Then everyone seemed to speak at once. Shanthala and Jagannath reprimanding Madhu. Priya replied in a hurt voice, "Why, I have no answer to that. He was older to my mother by fifteen years or so. He prevented her from becoming a nun. She joined the convent but because she fell in love with him more than her Christ, she married him. But God took him away early and punished her I suppose."

"Your religion preaches forgiveness, how can your God punish your mother for love?" Jagannath made sense at last. Shanthala was relieved, Priya was grateful. Madhu was miserable, she did not want to sympathize with this girl, and she just did not trust her. The little brother heard her and started his heart-wrenching kitten-like cry hallmark of hunger. Shanthala rushed to feed him and Priya got up to leave. Jagannath accompanied her to the car. He seemed to almost embrace her when he bid farewell. His wife watched from her room pensively. He came back and did not pick up his son.

"You could have been more gracious, you should teach your daughters some manners. Madhu behaves like a wild cat. The questions she asks, stupid buffoon."

"You behaved like a court jester, not her, she saved your face, and someone should think you have never seen an attractive girl in your life falling all over that girl, drooling."

"How dare you speak so cheaply? So what if I appreciate beauty? Is there a rule that a man can't even compliment a woman? She is fond of me."

"We have a son after three daughters, I have not even recovered from labor pains and tears and you want to lecture me on beauty. To think that I fell for your poems and that boyish smile which you flash for every other whore."

"She is not a whore, how dare you speak like that? She works hard from morning till evening, studying and earning her tuition fee."

Shanthala was furious, "She is not the mother of four children and has no philandering husband." Madhu, Mandakini and Meenu listened to the arguments from their room. Meenu was playing with Rita's hair. The doll was fixed by the watchman, but her hair was longer than Priya's. Meenu wanted to cut that hair to the same length as that of Priya.

Mandakini announced gravely, "This time they may actually divorce". She was two years older to Madhu, had an impressive vocabulary, and used high sounding words which she memorized from the dictionary. The word "divorce" was used frequently.

Just one year ago, they did not know the reason, he had not come home for weeks, then all relatives, uncles and grandparents had come, there was endless crying, angry tirades, chanting of the words, "What about the children?" Madhu was massively irritated with her aunt who stroked her head unnecessarily in a condescending manner befitting a would-be orphan. Mandakini's dictionary was used to find the meaning of the word "divorce" since she also did not know the meaning and was ashamed of her ignorance. Meenu had just learnt to walk and would tear the pages of any book, so she did not understand any of it.

Mandakini had solemnly declared that she would give tuitions to all the children and earn her livelihood. Madhu wanted to join the Venus circus and be a graceful dancer. She liked the clown, dwarf and the animals. Madhu worried about Meenu, it was not safe for someone so small. But Madhu actually liked the idea of being the brave child earning her living, jumping across the ropes and fire, to support her single mother. Then one day Jagannath would come to see the circus and would weep buckets when he saw the brave Madhu!

Mandakini would be petrified, morose, and irritable, she hated Madhu's theatrical approach to all problems. Madhu was guilty realizing that she should be sadder and not make elaborate plans for a bright future, like discussing what to do with the insurance money when someone has just died. But this year she also felt miserable, she had thought that with the entry of her brother, they would be a forever happy Colgate ad kind of family, everyone grinning all the time.

Meenu began to cry, saying that the hair of the doll must be cut immediately. Her cries were louder than the arguments in the next room. Mandakini wanted to silence her but Madhu let her cry, hoping that the duel would stop.

It did, Shanthala emerged asking what happened. Meenu was used to being the little darling she wept holding her mother. She wanted to sleep with her mother she said. But Shanthala gently refused, she was tired of placating the baby, and the fight with Jagannath. Madhu petted Meenu, kissed her hair, tried some jokes (imitating the clown in Venus circus) even agreed to let her cut Rita's hair. Meenu slept sobbing softly. Mandakini also fell asleep.

But Madhu could not sleep. She wanted to go to her cupboard of a dolls-house, her universe. Here she was a fairy with a magic wand. She had gathered there clouds cut out in a blue cardboard, with wisps of cotton stuck on them, houses made of cardboard boxes, one model house made in plywood from the architect's office, gardens of *ragi* plantation around them, huts made from cane baskets and water ponds in china bowls. It was a small world where all events were under her control. She had seven dolls bought by her maternal grandfather. They were closer to her than all her friends, as she knew their lives, dreams, fears, and she could alter their destinies.

She wanted to make Rita a nun, she had to stitch a white habit. Then this short hair, which was Meenu's supplication, could also be fulfilled. She picked her white kerchief and white ribbons and crept to her closet which was adjacent to her parent's bedroom. She opened the door of the closet quietly, it creaked. She got the scissors, and the cellophane tape, she could not stitch in the dark, with some street lights shining outside, and she could not find the eye of the needle. She cut the kerchief to the length of a long skirt and tried sticking it with the tape. The tape folded itself, it became a cord of some sort, she could not cut it with her scissors, and she needed a knife. Mariyamma would be asleep in the kitchen; she did not want to wake up that witch.

Then she heard the muffled sounds in the hall. Her father was talking over the phone. Did she imagine this? Or did she actually hear him laugh? Now she was really upset. How to get the knife? With the slightest noise he would know, he was already angry with her for that question. She always tried to be silent but somehow spoke what she should not speak. Each occasion was different, last time she had asked her father as he tore some pages wrongly typed by his typist in a fit of rage, that why was it wrong for Meenu to tear the pages but right for him to do the same. He had asked her to get out.

She decided to get the knife, so she crawled to the kitchen. She took the knife which was far away from Mariyamma, as she turned, she felt a crawling sensation on her forearm and screamed with horror involuntarily as she saw the creeping cockroach, above her wrist. Then Mariyamma screamed louder, and all hell broke loose.

Lights were switched on, Jagannath sat motionless in his seat. Mariyamma had switched on the kitchen light, Shanthala switched on the light in the hall. By the time Madhu explained Mariyamma that she was not possessed by any devil, she was making her doll a dress, so needed the knife, Jagannath had failed to explain to Shanthala what he was doing with the phone at that hour in the night. Shanthala stomped back to her bedroom, Jagannath slapped Madhu across her face. The slap was so loud, she felt faint. He did not even ask for an explanation. Madhu showed the doll mutely, trying to find words for what she felt. Jagannath picked up the doll, threw her down. Whatever dress that doll was wearing, was torn and the leg of the doll broke by that fall. Madhu was so horrified she just stood watching. Mariyamma tried to console, Madhu went to bed tearless, grateful that Meenu and Mandakini were asleep and did not watch her humiliation.

Next morning she woke up late. The first thought was "Something awful happened last night". Slowly events of the night were recalled. Meenu was also asleep; Madhu realized that Meenu had wet the bed. She never did that, was she imitating her brother? Did this mean she loved her as much as that little brother? Mother had told that it was a sure sign of profound love. Mariyamma appeared and drew the curtains apart. She touched Madhu's cheek with genuine sympathy, "A woman in puerperium with a son that too and this man wants to have girlfriends! Poor madam, poor child." Madhu hated pity. She went for her bath.

When she came out, Shanthala was interrogating Meenu about her bed wetting. Did she wake up in the night? Was she scared, what happened? Meenu was sitting on her mother's lap, silently. But as soon as she saw Madhu she asked, "Can I cut Rita's hair?" Madhu winced. Rita was lying on the floor of the hall, in a tattered dress with a broken leg. Madhu rushed, she could not let Meenu or anyone see this. Mariyamma would not talk, she hoped. She hid the doll behind the Krishna photograph in the showcase. It was a huge Painting depicting Krishna playing with the Gopikas. No one looked for anything lost, in the showcase.

Search meant looking in the corners, under the cot, in the darkness. No one searched in the open, nothing could be lost there. No one looked behind Gods.

The children got ready and went to school. Meenu had not joined the school yet, so she stayed back. Jagannath got up late and kissed Mandakini saying "Ta-Ta." He came near Madhu as though nothing had happened. Madhu walked away hurriedly, not daring to meet his eyes. Mandakini was tense about some unfinished homework, she sat in the car and did it diligently.

Madhu looked out of the window, at the disappearing mist, it was late December. She loved the mist, she wondered how to create it in her universe. That fragrant pieces of some wood called *Sambrani*, put in a small iron casket amidst burning coals, led to a cloud of thick smoke, it looked just like mist. But the mist was cold, and this smoke was hot. She thought her dolls would have to adjust. This entire exercise needed Mariyamma's cooperation, she mused. She would have to use that pity. That smoke was used to dry her brother's hair. Maybe she could put the burning coals, just two of them in that used, an empty tin of sweet corn soup which she had preserved for unknown multiple purposes.

They arrived at the school, Madhu joined her line. School pupil leader was absent, the girl who had to conduct the prayers before assembly had a sore throat. Madhu's class teacher came rushing to her, "Child, please sing on the stage, you are the only one I can think of who is so brave and at home on the stage". What did 'at home' mean, Madhu was not sure. She adored Sister Irene, her class teacher, and would do anything for her. She went on stage and started,

"Where the mind is without fear and the head is held high,
Into that heaven of freedom my father let my country awake.
Where knowledge is free, where words come out from the depths of truth."

To her dismay there was a lump in her throat every time she sang "father". She could not cry on stage, it was all to do with singing. Words could be recited with very little emotion. But while singing, feelings arrived without her permission, choking her with their power. The next prayer had to be in the national language.

'*Tum hi ho matha, pitha thumhi ho,* (Lord, "You are my mother, you are my father)
Tum hi ho bandhu, sakha tumhi ho… (You are my relative and my friend)

Tum hi ho sathi tum hi sahare, (You are my companion also my comfort)

Koi na apna seva tumhare..." (There is none other than you, whom I can call as my own")

She decided to camouflage her emotion as though she meant to express it, her voice shook betraying an orphan, but she pretended it was deliberate. She had no control over her emotional voice or her mobile face, she looked at Sister Irene. Irene had the look of profound appreciation, so she must be doing something right.

"Jo khil sakenge woh phul hum hain, (We are the flowers which can bloom)

Tumhari charano ki dhul hum hain... (I am the dust under your feet)

Daya ki drishti sada hi rakhna, (Let your kind eyes shine on me)

Tum hi ho bandhu sakha tum hi ho... (Forever, you are my relative, also my friend)

Madhu stepped down, the girl who was reading the newspaper came up. As she walked to her line, Sister Irene came near her, "God bless you, child. You are so devout." She crossed her forehead. Madhu suddenly asked, "Sister is it good to become a nun?" Sister Irene was surprised. "Why, yes of course! Did someone tell you it was bad?" Madhu was confused, why then Priya's father prevented her mother from becoming a nun?

Now her decision to make Rita a nun was strengthened, she was doing the right thing.

Madhu had problems with multiplication, in her arithmetic class. She did not like the symbol of multiplication, it was also used to denote wrong. How could one into one become one? One into zero becomes zero? One plus zero was still one, one minus zero was one, this she understood. She liked being accurate, being exact, but she thought about numbers, she liked some numbers. She liked them to be even. She liked pairs.

When she came home in the evening, the events of the night, returned to her mind. Shanthala, Meenu and the baby were all asleep. She found her doll behind the photograph where she had left it. She had to fix the right leg into a hole at the hip. She kept trying to push into the hole but was unsuccessful.

Her fingers became red and hurt with the prolonged effort. She decided to take Mariyamma's help. Mariyamma had deft hands, she bathed her tiny brother. Mariyamma was sitting in the verandah and smiled at Madhu.

"You want that doll to be repaired? Bring it here *Putti* (little girl) your poor mother is sleeping, don't disturb her." Madhu clenched her fists, Mariyamma was poor not her mother. "I wish this brother was not born.

What did he accomplish; everyone wanted him till he was born, now no one cares. Only mummy went through so much pain."

Mariyamma crossed her hands, touching her right cheek with left palm and left cheek with the right *"Shiva Shiva,* what a thing to say of your only brother. Pain is the essential ingredient of a woman's life. When you grow up you will know. Besides, you troubled your mother for one month with false pains, all the water was dried up. I wonder what you were doing for so long inside, playing with some dolls? Haha! There your doll is here." Madhu took Rita and wondered about what false pain was? She only knew true pain. How could any pain be false? Was there false pleasure too?

She was aware of false hair, false teeth, but she had never heard of false pain till now, and somehow she was associated with it. She did not want to be a part of falsity and cause pain to her mother. Shanthala carried the baby brother in a horizontal pose and came to the hall. Madhu asked her gravely, "Ma what is false pain? Did I hurt you more when I was born? Does it take longer for a girl to be born?" Shanthala was stunned. There was nothing false about the repeated bouts of pains she had endured when Madhu was being born. As though the baby did not want to see the world, she was reluctant to come out. The rains, her mother's arthritis, Jagannath had accepted some training schedule abroad, so he was absent then.

Shanthala said weakly, "I remember the pains, you don't as you were tiny. It must have been worse for you, you would have choked to death if you were not born when you did, and you made it luckily for me." Mother was so sweet as after all that pain she still wanted her, why? Madhu was overcome with gratitude.

She spent the evening doing her homework and painting her dolls. Her rubber dolls would be painted in different colors, unlike Rita they could not wear new clothes.

When Jagannath arrived later that evening there was tension at home. Nothing was natural about the interactions between Shanthala and him. Shanthala could not believe the innocence he boasted. Men seldom helped a pretty fatherless, unmarried girl, for purely humanitarian reasons. Shanthala was bitter, this was not the first time. Losing once was painful, to lose again and again, like dying, again and again, that was devastating. To touch a man who had laid with another willingly, even after she had given him all of her, that was humiliation.

Even her cells had united with his, multiplied into four children, what could another woman give him that she, Shanthala could not? What kind of hunger was that?

She had hugged her little girls for so many nights in his absence, imagining it to be him. She had longed for his male body to hold her, it was him always, even in her dreams. Why was it different for him then? Maybe she did not know how to love a man.

Shanthala did not want proof of betrayal, she wanted to believe him. But being devout and with children all the time she could believe only the truth. The conviction of her marriage was her children.

But marriage had to stand on one conviction, that made everything bearable, every pain a joy, that madness called love. That joy of waking up with him day after day, and that restless need to put her head on his chest at nights. Not wanting to move despite the numbness when he slept on her lap. That head reeling gush of emotions when he uttered her name even in sleep. Those early days before the birth of children when they watched 'Sound of Music' and jumped all the benches of Cubbon park singing, 'I am sixteen going on seventeen'.

The first time they had gone shopping for vegetables and she was lost in the streets of the city market, crying helplessly when he pinched her waist from the back and passed that mischievous smile, biting a raw carrot. If she was not so relieved to find him she would have chopped his head. Then once when he wanted to go to Bhimsen Joshi's concert, they had no money and she had collected all the old newspapers, sold them and got just enough money for one ticket, fighting over who should go they had both stayed at home, in the middle of the night listening to some ancestral drums, had exhausted each other with the simple ancient entertainment of sensual love.

Dinner was made by Mariyamma, Shanthala served food in spite of her pains. Children were silent, especially Madhu. The telephone rang making her nervous. Jagannath quietly got up with his plate and continued a low tone conversation with that silly smile on his face. Shanthala feigned indifference. She knew his arguments, justifications by memory. She was only intelligent, not an intellectual like him. He used his intellect like a license to explain his transgressions.

His friends won literary awards, writing poems about some woman's breasts and hips, unfulfilled desires of a child widow, extramarital sex of a woman with an impotent husband, always the man was a benefactor bestowing sex on a woman. Their wives seemed more unfulfilled, which they did not seem to notice. Wives accompanied the husbands when he received his awards, his concubine or concubines sat next to him on the dais.

Oh, it was the rain, mist, mood, and two bodies glistening with perspiration, how natural! Nude painting exhibition, ceramic models of sexual poses, the endless talk about colors, texture, light etc., bullshit, horse shit all the shit in the world.

This constant whipping of human emotions, to unknown heights, wallowing in senses, indulgence, licentiousness that is all it was. What was he seeking she did not know, she did not care anymore. She went to her bedroom, with her baby.

Jagannath made the divan in the hall as his bed, a huge mosquito net around the top of the divan was put. Jagannath was telling Meenu the story of a one-eyed giant who fell in love with a mermaid. The giant learnt to sing from a sea-gull and sang every night, hoping to lure the mermaid. The song was like a cry, soulful, got better with every night. Mermaid listened to him from under the ocean, sometimes there was a harp in her heart echoing his song. One night the giant lost his optimism, his heart broke and unable to bear the pain of unrequited love he stopped singing. Mermaid missed his voice. She could not sleep without hearing him, she wriggled in the water, came up to find the giant was dying. She kissed him in the moonlight and the giant got his second eye, then every full moon night the giant and the mermaid met and the song of their love made the ocean rise. Meenu slept and was put into her bed by Jagannath.

Madhu sat up with the white kerchief on the dining table, with the two pieces which had to be stitched to make a dress. Jagannath came and sat on one of the chairs. "What are you doing?" No reply. "It looks like a dress, can I help?" No reply. He got up to go, then Madhu spoke, "Where did you read that story? Is that book in our house?" Jagannath smiled sheepishly, "I made it up by myself." Madhu now felt that the value of the story was diminished. That was a tender age when only truth appealed, adults supposedly knew the truth and told the truth, only children lied. As though he read her mind Jagannath said, "Every story is someone's imagination. Nothing true about it, just because it is printed somewhere, doesn't make it true."

Madhu stitched the dress at a furious pace, hurriedly. The needle pricked her finger, a small drop of blood oozed staining the cloth of her doll. Jagannath involuntarily took her hand in his and went to the medicine cabinet got a circular bandage and put it around her finger. "Are there no mermaids then? Was that also a lie?" Jagannath thought for a while, "If you go to sleep, you will see her in your dreams." Madhu vaguely understood. "So she is real in the dream world?" Jagannath nodded, "Yes, that world is far away, very few fortunate people go there, but if they do she is there, really."

Madhu smiled with relief, she knew how to go there, she just had to imagine. "Goodnight papa" he hugged and kissed her. But when she turned back she saw him alone inside that net it looked like a cage. She came back, "You are the only one sleeping alone, is this only for this night?" Jagannath said, "I am the man, I am not scared of cockroaches, nor devils." But there was something in his eyes almost like despair, something far worse than fear.

Jagannath looked helplessly alone and avoided her scrutinizing glance, like a little boy hiding his wound from mother. She went back to her bed, wanting to go to some other faraway world, she hoped she could make Rita a mermaid. When she fell asleep she heard endless chanting of the waves. The ocean was in her eternal dance with all the waves, big and small, all her children. She saw bubbles of water likc prayer beads, broken loose from a rosary, surrounding the mermaid. She was beautiful, with a narrow waist, fishy tail. The foam of lashing waves was surrounded by a cold mist. She was singing in the moonlight a kind of song sounding like a cry of the sea-gull. There was no giant in sight. At the end of one wave, another wave was born. The lonely shore of endless sand almost like a dessert cupped the waves.

Madhu realized after several decades that Jagannath never strayed. He always loved Shanthala.

~***~

5. love letters with spelling mistakes

~~~~~~~~~~~~~~~~***~~~~~~~~~~~~~~~

July 4, 1995 – Tuesday Evening

In the living room, the bookcase contained Oxford dictionaries and Encyclopedias of social sciences by Will Durant. One book 'Jean Genet' by Sartre half-read was seated behind her. Sindhu sang *raag* Purya Dhanashri, strumming *tanpura,* taking *aalap* with her eyes closed. It was evening as a warm glow streamed through the old fashioned windows. Curtains fluttered; there was a lamp next to an idol of Vishnu in five metals in a small niche in the wall.

Tara walked in tiptoeing. Her white apron on the shoulders, a bag slung on the other side… there was a newspaper packet in her hands. She sank on the sofa wanting to absorb the music. Her mind was floating over in a disciplined range of classical music. After spending the whole day in controlling deranged emotions, it was a relief to let go of one's own emotions… if only in a tune… *aalap* deepening the experience… mild variations of the octaves working up to a frantic climax. Sindhu stopped and looked at Tara, "When did you come in?"

Tara remained speechless for it was a sort of betrayal to hear spoken words when one was listening to another language of pure emotion. She recovered, saying she did not wish to disturb the music as it was healing.
~~~~~~~~~~~~~~~~

"Healing is your job," laughed Sindhu. Mother had gone somewhere, not a sound in the house, perhaps to the temple. Sindhu was curious about the newspaper packet in Tara's hands. Tara was evasive and it got all the more attention that was somehow shaming to Tara.

"It probably is a gift from some grateful patient in the loony bin why shouldn't I see?" Sindhu knew to annoy Tara. "Please do not address the psychiatric hospital by that slang." Sincerity was not an act; she disliked hearing any sort of ridicule against the patients or the hospital.

"I am not going to be politically correct in the privacy of our home. It could be a gift such as a new shade of lipstick, wilting wine or chocolate caramel to impress that Dilton Doyle?" Now, Tara really had enough. "Oh stop it; we just happen to be in the same batch. Being the only girl in this batch of students, I had to find a mild and almost a Forrest Gump as a friend, so that I know the schedule of classes arranged all of a sudden, new journal, a research project etc." That would end the exploration, thought Tara.

"Freud would say you have repressed sexuality to hang around with the most boring guy who is least threatening to you sexually and you are the biggest sexual challenge to him. "The way, he dotes on every word that falls out of your blessed lips... as if he has only 'Plato' feelings for you?" Tara knew that Sindhu was unapologetic about her observations, maybe she was right. But then, her own feelings mattered.

She felt none of it for this friend. She took people at face value, refused to read between the lines of every guy she met, he was truly a decent man. It was impossible to imagine him in any act except that of a sincere student afraid of exams. He would probably marry a girl if her marks cards had good grades. His first symptom of affection is "How can I let you miss these classes, you may fail your exams."

Tara smiled to herself, recalling how shocked she was when she first learnt about the sexual act. And how she had imagined every decent married man without clothes doing that with his wife and could not bear to look at him after that.

Sex was neither natural nor a dominating instinct for her. She was not even curious about it. Men were nicer to her so it was easy to be friends with a man. The way women were absolutely nice to her in the face and somehow spoke in a way that betrayed her totally, later she bit her lip…hurt.

Sindhu was sister fully different. She was quite perseveringly curious about the paper packet, Tara recoiled from her touch. Now, Sindhu got concerned and the paper packet fell out of Tara's lap revealing the contents. There were bottles of Mediker and Lycil in it. Sindhu was surprised, "In your hair?! Dilton gave you these, two packets of knowledge, with one packet of lice?"

Tara spoke calmly, "His name is Pradeep. Stop calling him by Archie's Comics character. I got these from my patient Shanthi in the chronic ward. A burnt-out case of Schizophrenia, she is such a docile and gentle soul, muttering to herself. She does not make eye to eye contact with anyone. But once a month a barber comes to shave her head, she gets very violent. Last week, he came in when I was in the wards and I told him not to shave. I thought I could get her to wash her hair. Last week I met her four times, as I was trying to get her to tell me her residential address.

I want to send letters to her family. She was abandoned fifteen years ago during a time she was very disturbed, so the police brought her to the psychiatric hospital by a reception order from the magistrate. In her lucid intervals, she talks about a girl child. Husband may have remarried in all probability, but her child must be a grown-up adult by now if in some way they could include her in their family home it would be helpful for her future. So, I must have got these parasites on my head from her. Please do not say this to mom; she will be irritated that I chose Psychiatry."

"Lousy girl! I will not speak about it if you promise not to tell mother about my visit to the country club with George," Tara frowned. George was a Pink Floyd fan strumming the guitar claiming to be a Jazz musician. Mother came in carrying a bag of flowers, "How long does it take for you girls to come to the door? Did you eat something? Did your father call?" Tara took the bag peering inside and replied laughingly, "One question at a time, if you had set the Common Entrance Test, there would have been six hundred questions instead of sixty and I am not hungry."

"Being with the mentally ill the whole day does this to you. That beautician in Sparsh Parlor says that after massaging our bodies all the heat goes into her and she too needs to oil herself to bring down the heat. Whole day listening to sob stories, at the end you are home crying as though there is something wrong with your life." There was a relief in the reductionist approach to life. Mother was a specialist in this right brain, totalitarian philosophy. She had a therapeutic distance from the subject of interest; she had been an advocate of obstetrics and gynecology, about how normal it was to assist deliveries.

But Tara was more depressed in those wards, as though being a woman justified that interest. The doctor, nurse, patient, ayah were all women. But women continued to judge the sexual choices, reproductive choices of other women through the lens of a man!

Ayahs commenting about what a fuss this or that woman made to push the baby, how absolutely pampered & spoilt, and even telling the woman how she must have enjoyed the act, then she could spread her legs! Tara was so completely repulsed by the attitude of women towards other women! Perhaps animals were kinder to another animal in pain.

They did not use language to assault another who was already in pain. Just because the zygote was carried by an organ called uterus in the woman's body, the sole creative responsibility was bestowed on her! Albeit negatively, in all the proud moments it was the surname, the first name was impolite and the only sir mattered. It completely threw Tara. Children did not inherit maladies quietly, at least they wanted to say that the world they were born in was imperfect - at least a poetic license to say that!

Sindhu had readily agreed and conceded that man and woman should have taken turns in having babies. Mother was still a bit angry about psychiatry. Those who reached the asymptomatic phase of remission seldom acknowledged the disease, let alone the doctor! For her, everything was about popularity and in this field of medicine there was a shroud of silence. It could never be as impersonal as caring for a kidney or an artery; it was always personal, confidential. If practiced perfectly no one should know.

"Last month, a mad man slapped you and your professor tells you that a student should be slapped several times to show that she worked in the wards before she gets a master's degree, what if someone rapes you?" "Stop, if you look at it that way, no place is safe. Not even the grandfather's house where you used to send us every holiday. At least here there are security guards." Mother was defensive about her father's house that to her was safer than any house. Tara did not explain.

July 5, 1995 – Wednesday Morning

Tara sat in the outpatient clinic of the psychiatric hospital. She looked at Pradeep, a short man, bespectacled, and he did look a bit like Dilton Doily, thought Tara. He was reticent, smiled at her shyly, "I posted that letter of yours to Shanthi's house at Kansur. It is a village in Malnad district, Sagar Taluk."

"You improvised the address I hope. Thanks!" Tara could depend on him. He was a bit troubled, saying, "Are you okay?" Tara was perplexed, "Why shouldn't I be?"

"That Dr. Prasad called you alone for a case discussion in the evening at half-past six, you should be careful with him around, he has a bad reputation." Tara laughed with embarrassment, she had not gone in the evening, she told him she was busy and would discuss the case in the lunch hour.

He would tell tales about her to the professor, portray her as careless, not interested to do her work and so on. It had happened before with many others. Finally, it was her reputation that would be questioned, not his or any of his predecessors. Jung was all wrong about entropy, no matter how many times she tried to change her mind about the unfair sex… it continued to play the same game. Either there were Pradeeps who were so uncomfortable with their sexuality that she felt like a case of trance or possession disorder taken over by Mother Goddess. Or there were overconfident Don Juan's for whom conquest was mandatory, not the intimacy.

For them taking a woman to bed was like getting a medal in a war among men. Invariably some other diffident man was lusting after her and it was important to show him his place by getting her. So, it was essentially a disturbing relationship with other men. Men of her own age merely treated her as competition, irritated that older men from whom they wanted to curry favors, gave her more attention.

So, all her intelligence merely made them mistrust her… the smart men wanting a prettier girl with lesser brains and the smart women wanted handsome men without brains. Perfect matches made! Like John Nash's games theory. She was the blonde, could not get a single eligible man… in a world where mediocrity below the norm and above the norm were both not normal.

Pradeep was surprised, "Why? I mean how did you manage that?" Actually, she had given him more credit than he deserved; he was a man who could only be affected by another man impinging on his possession. He would not bother even for a second if he had his own girlfriend, whatever may happen to Tara. Injustice was affecting only when it affected him. Otherwise, he could even use it to his advantage.

Tara kept an even voice, "I have my strategies to deal with unwanted attention." "It may not work each time." Prasad entered and Tara was flustered. She said, "Good morning! Sir."

He did not want respect. "Do not knight me; I am not exactly 100 years old." She kept quiet. When he wanted to hit on a girl, age was not exactly attractive. Or else he did not mind the power it conferred on him. Professor Velliyappan went across to his room… so, all were silenced. The hierarchy was rigid in this setup.

The first patient in the outpatient clinic came in with his case file. Tara entered his file number in the record, looked up to hear the patient introduce himself as Venkatesh Pillai from Kerala, a school teacher for twenty-five years in Ernakulum.

She asked, "Are you married?" It was just to enter the socio-demographic data in the records. He was hesitant, "No madam, recently I wanted to..." She sensed a discomfort that was palpable, so trying to not sound very curious; she asked casually, "Any specific reason?" He replied nonchalantly, "I love children." Somehow his answer was not casual; it belied an intensity that she tried to douse..." Obviously! You work with them."

"No madam, not like that. Not the way you think." Now, there was no circumventing of the problem, she stopped writing and said, "Please elaborate." He said, he liked touching them, holding them and loving them in an unabashed, 'Holier than thou' attitude. Tara had to ensure that her face was devoid of expression of horror she felt inside. He clarified that he was attracted to children younger than grade 5. She wanted to know what exactly this "love" was...

"What did you do?" "It is never about me, it is always what they want." "How can you know what they want? I don't understand."

"I will explain doctor. I teach only primary school. When I get interested in a child I look out for little signs which show that the child is also interested in me." Tara prodded, "like…? Give me specific examples."

He cleared his throat and started to really explain, he was probably a good teacher. They tell that rhyme *twinkle twinkle little star* looking at me in a special way. Sometimes, they ask me permission to go to the toilet with a smile; it is not the same every time. Like this girl, Rupa gave all the chocolates in a box for her birthday into my hands instead of distributing to all the children.

"So you thought that she was interested in you." Hopefully, this was Socratic questioning meant to shed some insight.

He was angry, "She was interested!" Tara realized it was a mistake to upstage the sainthood act and said, "Sorry for interrupting please continue sir."

He took the bait, "Then I make friendship with the girl, ask her about her family, friends, places she has gone to, movies she has seen." Tara asked, "Is it only girls?"

He was trying to be honest or was so oblivious to the world? "Both madam. Boys are less interested in love, so I don't love them so often, once in a while that is all for a change." Tara braved it. "Continue please."

"By talking and friendship, I make sure they are fully pure and innocent. That is they don't have any idea about sex and such matters. Some mothers have only one child and they come to the school all the time, I don't take such children as they don't need much loving, you see? Then I ask them to write a letter to someone they love the most or write two lines about anything they love. That gives me a clue as to how to love them. Like this girl wrote to her puppy named Hobbs. I read Calvin and Hobbs for her sake and told her all of it. She really liked the stories. I called myself as Calvin. Do you want to see her letter? *(He opens the briefcase and removes hundreds of letters, with childish scrawls)* I hope you don't mind, they have many spelling mistakes, she is small, you know. I feel responsible as I am also their English teacher."

"What did you do to her?"

"Last period in school is sports or Physical education. So I took her with me to the sports materials storage room. It is in the basement and is quite dark, so I lit it up in candles and there I licked her all over, and soft puppy bites and asked her to copy me. She really cried with pleasure. She was beautiful, so pure, no hair or blobs of flesh like grown-up bitches."

"Sorry to interrupt again but I'll just come back in a minute." She went to a corner wiped her face in a kerchief drank some water and returned.

"So how many children have you loved till date?"

"About two hundred. I have one hundred and sixty letters here, some with drawings also."

"What about your family? Parents, brother, sister, where are they? And you love the children and they love you, so why did you come to this Hospital?"

"I have no father, my mother brought me up. She was a good mother but a very bad woman. She did dirty things for money, went with all kinds of men. She loved me the most in this world as I was the only pure person in her life. She told me I should always remain pure, and not become like her or the men who visited her. She died when I was twelve and I was put in an orphanage. One older boy loved me and took care of me; I have remained pure to this day."

Tara persisted, "Why did you come to the hospital?" "I met this Hindi teacher, Elena is her name. She came to our school one year ago. She was very white and pure always praying and all. She is about thirty-five years or so and not married. She talked to me on her own, told me she was alone with her old mother. She said

I should get married as I need someone to look after me. She said love inside a marriage is also pure and divine. And I suspect she wanted to marry me, but I saw little Rima who newly joined grade 2nd, she needed my love.

She fell down in the playground and came to the storage room herself asking for a bandage. I was kissing her down there when Elena saw me. She said terrible things to me, and she said she will complain about me to the Principal and Rima's mother too. I told her I have never had actual sex with any child or adult. I have just rubbed my fellow on them, asked them to hold that is all. She kept saying that I was sick, sick and sick and needed to see a psychiatrist. I did not want to go to a doctor in Kerala, news spreads fast there; they may think that I am mental and dismiss me you know. I don't know if I am a patient."

Tara asked, "Tell me sir one last question. Do you want to marry Elena?"

"I love children; I don't think that what I do is sick. I am not hurting these children, only loving them. How can that be wrong? She called me horrible names said that I would burn in hell, she said I was sick. She said she will hand me over to the police. Please tell me if I am sick and need treatment, I don't want to marry that bitch. But I always want to be healthy or else I will lose my job. I don't want to be scared, I want to be brave. My friend in the hostel showed me some papers where they said homosexuality was not wrong some men love men if that is okay why not love children?"

Tara sounded really upset, "Sir I think you do have a problem which needs to be treated urgently. Since you don't belong to this city, it is better you get admitted for the treatment. Sir since a child is not mature sexually or otherwise to give consent to you for a sexual involvement; it is a crime socially, morally and in the eyes of law. So you need the treatment."

She thought, she needed guidance and went to the professor. Professor and Prasad were talking sitting down. Tara knocked on the door and entered. Professor motioned her to sit down, looked at her expectantly. Tara was shaken, "Can I discuss my case, Sir?" Professor seemed to sense her discomfort, "Anything unusual? What is the diagnosis?"

Tara blurted out in relief, "Disorder of sexual preference... paraphilia... Pedophilia" Professor seemed casual. "You can discuss with Dr. Prasad, he is an authority on all sexual disorders (laughs) except for erectile dysfunction." Prasad feigned embarrassment, "Sir please, not in front of juniors."

Tara said in a very cold voice, "He is a pedophile sir; he has abused two hundred children, so I asked for admission." Professor asked, "Why admission?" It was the routine. "You know nothing. All decisions will be made by us. We are here to show your inadequacy." Tara said, "He is from Kerala, has no place to stay anyway for treatment. If he goes back without taking therapy he may abuse more children." *[India did not have a law for mandatory reporting or arrest of pedophiles then. Protection of Children from Sexual Offenses Act was passed in 2012, 17 years later.]*

Professor made light of her protest, "You sound more like a public prosecutor rather than a doctor." Tara decided to stick to her guns, "I strongly feel he is more guilty than insane." Professor said seriously, "Have you heard the Hippocrates oath madam? Do you know what the attitude of a therapist towards the patient must be?"

Tara argued "Sir, there is a potential for treatment I am not disputing that. He was reared by a single parent, a mother who was a commercial sex worker. So there was no role model of a father. He has an erroneous set of sexual beliefs, cognitive therapy for that, aversive therapy for child-related stimuli; covert conditioning is to be attempted. He may have some sexual dysfunctions that need to be addressed. His heterosexual skills must be assessed, improvised if need be. He needs assertiveness training. But first, he should stop abusing the children." Professor seemed annoyed.

"So are you going to the police by any chance? Do you know that what you have is privileged information?" Tara was furiously indignant, "Sir, if an HIV positive patient tells me that he is going to have sex with his girlfriend, it is not privileged information. I can discreetly warn her. I should inform the school authorities." Professor lost his temper, "He will lose his job don't you realize? No life is at stake here, he is after all admitted to the hospital, and your patient is in front of you, so treat him. The society will take care of itself". She could not believe her ears.

Tara replied, "After all, prison gives the best aversive therapy. Every crime has an explanation which does not justify its occurrence, he should be punished and if we can help the judiciary, why not?"

Professor interrogated her, "Has he raped a child?" Tara said, "No sir. But he might have ..."

"Then Dr. Tara you are wasting my time as this case is not legally admissible. *(In a kinder but firm tone)* Maybe it would be good if you explore your own psyche to find out what is causing such an exaggerated reaction from you".

"You can talk to Dr. Meera you can be comfortable with her. Tara said, "Sir I don't think my reaction is really exaggerated if you see those innocent letters, love letters he calls them," there was a lump in her throat, her voice breaking…

"Let us discuss this case tomorrow in the grand rounds. Meanwhile, Dr. Prasad will help you." Tara said under her breath, "I don't need any help."

She chose not to look at Dr. Prasad, who would merely feel legitimized in his emotional abuse. She felt rage, here in this hospital, psychiatrists prided on analyzing all lofty or noble human emotions as pathological and requiring help.

They were anti-Darwin in their theory of human evolution. The only true emotions for them were sex or anger and hunger. Basically to be selfish was normal. Anything else was abnormal. Actually, they had no problem with sex; their problem was lack of it… Any preference was acceptable, not the abstinence. Their justification of the primitive and suspicion towards any evolved emotion saddened Tara. It made her doubt her choice of psychiatry… Like Vasco-Da-Gama, maybe she was in the wrong place.

There were no answers for all these questions. Her so-called peers, as usual, were happy with depersonalization; they accepted being mere bundles of instincts. Some became more ruthless in their pursuit of pleasure. They wanted to affirm their 'Normality' by becoming conformist to a fault.

It was a matter of a few months, a degree and a job, before Pradeep would avidly embrace conformity and make a sexual choice… Tara knew the most servile survived the best. Since they were never tested, all tests were to induce servility and to homogenize the unequal.

July 6, 1995 – Thursday Morning

The next afternoon after the grand rounds, outside the hospital premises Pradeep and Tara sat discussing. Pradeep felt Tara should not have back answered the professor, that too in the grand rounds in front of everyone. That man could get difficult; she seemed to have too many convictions and stood up for all of them. Yes… as an afterthought, Tara was plagued by self-doubt.

"He doesn't want me to inform the school authorities. If you were treating a rare case of Rabies the first thing to do is isolate the patient, is it not? First do no harm is the principle he says. What about those little children waiting to be mauled by this man? How to prevent them from getting hurt? He says that I am overreacting, better still, he calls it attention-seeking behavior, as though I have not had enough of unwanted attention in this place."

"Do you really think that he came to the hospital to protect himself from the police in a case that Elena informs a parent and takes him to Jail?"

Tara was scared, "He can plead insanity then you see it is possible. I find it hard to believe that living in human society for so long he does not know that sexual overtures towards a child are morally wrong. Then why should he do it stealthily in the storage basement, not choose a child whose parent is over-involved in school? I find his explanations to be too contrived, made up. Recidivism is the rule in sexual crimes. I know he has convinced himself that sex with a grown-up woman is impure or some such thing. I don't doubt that his upbringing had a lot to do with it. But if you dig every crime as a psychiatrist you will find a thousand contributing factors to classify it as abnormal behavior… so scrap the judiciary and treat them all in a mental hospital simple." She was sarcastic; it was not possible to be humane with a grown man and inhuman towards a child.

Pradeep tried to be sensible… To prove that he actually abused a child was not easy; parents in India would not come forward to a court.

"Children can't be verbal about this, you know that there may be bed wetting, tantrums, sudden scholastic backwardness, n number of illnesses but not even a single child can cogently verbalize it. The only witness is Elena and what if she turns hostile? But he can turn the tables and file defamation against the hospital management."

Tara was worried, the man had another 13 years of service, 10 children per year, and another 130 children could be abused. She was not able to sleep last night recalling his exploits and those innocent love letters. He had such erroneous set of beliefs about women, sex; he had lived this for the past twenty years and he was not going to change in ten days of therapy even if the great Dr. Velliappan did it. And the teacher wanted to keep the job.

"Then all the more reason to believe that he won't lose it so easily." If he has pretended to have no insight, evinced no guilt just to plead some kind of insanity he may be tutored by a lawyer already. Tara said, "I am sure if he was interrogated by the police he may have said something else. Listen, what if we contact Elena?" Pradeep was irritable. "And tell her what, Tara? Take him to the police, get him dismissed? What makes you think she will oblige? Be practical." Tara felt really down.

Mentally challenged children remained that way. Demented patients only got worse; Schizophrenics treated for positive symptoms developed negative symptoms. Treat them for anxiety, they came back with depression. Treat depression they became manic, alcoholics forever relapsed, what was she doing here? And here she thought, at last, she could make a difference and save at least some children and that also seemed impossible. Why was it that her mom was always right?

Pradeep was pragmatic… "Treat it as just a case why should you get into the savior robe? It is a job like any other at the end of the day. Your job is to treat the patient that is it."

Tara could not… "You remind me of my maid. When I show her a stain on a dress which she should have washed, she tells me I washed it, if it has not gone what should I do? She thinks her job is to wash, not to clean the fabric. How can we say the same, we treated the case but he did not get any better, and what can we do? (Sarcastic) Yes he told me he likes having oral sex with second standard kids but I thought I treated the case, maybe he did not recover fully so he abused some more children. Let me try once again."

Pradeep gave up exasperated… "Well, I can't help you, Tara. No one can." Tara looked down. Pradeep was concerned, "Please don't cry, that won't help anyway." Tara muttered, "Who cries because it helps? You cry when you can't do anything else." Pradeep tried, "Shall I write some anonymous letters to the principal and tell him to verify with Elena, It may make them suspicious and our pal may get caught in the act."

Tara felt doing something was better than crying. "I would not have thought of this... thanks. You are becoming official Pradeep Mail Service." "I probably have a recessive gene carrying dissocial traits." He said...

Tara knew he was imitating the letters he was posting to the unresponsive Shanthi's family.

(Six years ago)
September 18, 1989 - Monday
It had stopped being an ordinary month......
She could no longer write her diary. Writing a diary was returning to self after mixing with everyone and everything. And when he is at home, how to return to self? Did acupressure cure pins and needles? She saw his eyes everywhere. Heard him laugh in the kitchen, mom spoke in her dialect animatedly, "What to cook?"

I am from Madras, I love sambar... Auntie's dosa with many holes, he played up to mom. Dad seemed happy to be left alone. Her relatives... Had she not entertained his relatives? She switched on the radio in her room, a low murmur of a grandiose voice... a radio jockey full of him-self... attitude. She had kept a low volume.

After building a house, it was often about who are all on dad's side and who are all on mom's side. Dad's side relatives, the suckers… mom's side relatives the waifs. Mom mixed the colors in the right proportions before she made a Rangoli for the Gods.

He behaved like a brother in the kitchen, while seated in the living room. She was preparing to go to college. She thought of Abdul, was she wrong? Maybe going to his uncle's house to say she was not interested. But she wanted privacy to make him understand, she did not want to hurt him. She had gone to his uncle's house, to tell him that she can't accept his love letter. Her father had read the love letter…

"If a low-class Muslim boy, a Jataka Sahib (a horse carriage driver) can write a love letter to you, I can imagine how cheap your conduct must have been." But the meeting had not gone the way she planned at all.

As she tried to find words… *I like you, but it's not love… I never once imagined myself as your girlfriend or anything… I cannot, even if I tried…* he had put his arms around her. He smelt of smoke, and next, his mouth was on hers. He gave her a long wet kiss. She was so surprised. It felt very soft, tender and private.

How did he know to do this? It did not feel cheap. It felt very intimate. Not violent. Not scary. Not at all intrusive. She was confused. She liked the kiss, liked the fact that he felt like doing this… but she did not think him to be intelligent or refined or cultured.

She looked at him, he was ordinary. How did he do this? He presumed she liked him. But she liked the kiss only. How to be dishonest? The kiss was not a simple matter. It did not need love to enjoy a kiss?! Maybe she was like that. Cheap? After that day, their interactions were not simple. He wanted affirmation of whatever had occurred, in a look or a word. She was weary. Nothing had changed. It was just a feeling in the lips and she did not want to love him because of one kiss.

He neither knew Jane Austen nor knew Keats, definitely no Sartre, he had never even thought about existential angst. He did not think much, no confusion, no despair, no metaphysical doubts, and no moral complications. He could not play the guitar nor dance, he was neither an orator nor an actor, and he was not even a mug pot who got good marks by rote memory. He was just an ordinary boy. He had no problem in being attracted to her or kissing her suddenly. He knew to do these things… he could do it, in a way that caused her no shame. She tried to brush it aside. But either he did something to remind her or she recalled it more often than Shelley.

And sometimes when she saw him laughing with his studious boyfriends whose grades matched with hers, she was afraid if he would talk about that kiss? Maybe they also would think her to be cheap? But he had not. No one else showed anything different. He met her in practical's they were partners in the labs. He was less aggressive than before, tolerated her superior knowledge more easily… as though he had swallowed it.

"Will you take your cousin to college library? He needs to study for the PG entrance; he will pick up some books." Mom asked. She nodded.

He seemed smug. Five years ago she was merely twelve. They had not met after that, not alone. She was wearing skirts those days, just a petticoat inside. She felt more clothed, less exposed now.

Yet, he had a way of looking. They sat in one auto to go to her college. She was careful; to keep her legs straight and away from him, hold on to the sidebar so as to not shake on the speed breakers. "You grow more beautiful each time I see you." She did not reply. "So the rouge in your cheeks, kohl in your eye… didn't you dress up a little more today? Because of me?"

"This dress is a bit tight." She was polite. "I have no cosmetics except for kohl, and this dress was bought last year, hence a bit tight. In fact today I am sloppy, usually, I look better." She did not defend the flush.

"So, how is college?" She did not say anything. They reached. He did not pay the auto driver, she did. As usual, Abdul saw her before she saw him and he walked up to her. He thought the guy next to her was a stranger.

"Hi, you are late today... my favorite color!" His smile was quickly hidden as the stranger introduced himself, "I am her brother." She corrected, "Cousin, mother's sister's son"

"Oh..." Abdul tried to depict the distance of a casual acquaintance. But those two minutes of unconscious camaraderie was not missed. Her cousin spoke quickly. "I will go with your friend to the library. He will show me around, easier done by him. Don't you think?" She retreated. Should she be relieved or tense?

Now even college seemed unsafe. She had one place away from all the unpredictability of home, but he had spoiled that, would be spoiling even the library. It was over. Nowhere to go...

Abdul missed the first two hours. When he came to the lab he seemed to look at her newly, as though he did not know her.

"Why did you not tell anything about him to me before?" Mild accusation? She had even told him about her dog. "I did not see the need to talk about him; I have not met him in five years." "Yeah, he told me." Was there an embarrassed smile on Abdul's face… or did she imagine it?

They were unusually quiet together. He did use the pipette to put alkali into the acid as they waited for the pink color, titrating drop by drop. The taste was bitter… or sour. Every drop, he looked at her. She felt evaluated. It was sort of devaluated… whatever happened in two hours?

Abdul was not important to her. He was pleasant. Sometimes when she dressed, he could look at her like a man who had seen nothing else or no one else. There was undeniable tension… she had managed to rouse something in him; it was stronger than anything around him or in him. She was becoming dependent on the effect she had on him. She felt alive, yet safe in his eyes. Now, it had gone.

He seemed destroyed. He kind of looked at her body parts impersonally, like they were a part of some scheme. She looked questioningly when the color turned pink and he wrote the reading in the record book, flinching as her finger touched his. She could not fathom the change in two hours.

"Are you okay?" She hesitated near the door.

He said, "Yea… your cousin or brother or relative left in a bus. He wanted to meet me tomorrow…"

She was speechless. No, she could not talk about the relative here. She did not want to talk about him at all, to anyone. She never wanted him in her house. She did not want him in her college. She did not want him anywhere near her. Now, it seemed Abdul had to be told something. She was determined to be silent. Nothing had happened. There was nothing to tell. He was not her brother.

She found an auto. She did not want to go home, yet that was the only address she remembered. He was in the living room chatting with her sister; she went upstairs to her room, locked the door. Switched on the stereo, "While my guitar gently weeps…" Time seemed to pass very slowly.

When she came out of the room, her father was watching the news. She sat next to him, he patted her head… she might have to speak. Would she know what words to use to explain what he did?

Her cheeks felt hot, even her ears… it felt like it happened yesterday. He spoke about some prime minister and his unintelligible choice of words. He should read a dictionary first, he should know the tenses… simple, past, and past perfect… her father went on. She became more diffident… past imperfect tense… she would have to refer the dictionary but she knew the anatomical terms for all body parts by now. The hidden, ugly, small or big… but actions… what to say to that? No, that was not a kiss… opening of the mouth… forcible opening of the mouth… she kept thinking hard. She would write them down.

He slept in the hall. She closed her doors but did not sleep. During the day, it was not possible to see the hour hand move over the clock as time happened to pass. In the night, it was possible to see it move. When one stopped seeing they could feel the moves. She heard his movements on the bed in the hall. She was convinced that it could not go on like this. He would stay in her house till PG entrance exams and that was three months! He may come to college every day. No, she had to act… she had to speak… she had nowhere else to go… the room… yes, but she could not lock herself every evening.

The next day he was ready as she climbed down the stairs. "So, you are coming with me every day?" He smiled, "Of course. I came to Bangalore to be with you." She stared, his father was retiring soon, he had built a house in Bangalore… It really had nothing to do with her. He sometimes said he was her brother, even now after all that he had done. Maybe he did it to his own sister too. All brothers did not do the things he did. She was sure of it. She could complain about his behaviour. But what if no one believed her? It was very difficult to say those things in public. Mom liked him, she knew that.

He put his arm around her, she started… "No!" He laughed… "Oh, so you listen to Beatles, have boyfriends and won't want me putting an arm around you?" She stiffened. "I have no boyfriend." He merely looked at her quizzically… "I see. You have acquired many new things… habits…"

She was afraid if he spoke about the cheap kiss to dad? Abdul would not have told, or would he? His arm stayed on her shoulders, his fingers fiddled her bra strap. "I have my secrets too…" She shrugged off his hands. She stared back at him, "Do not touch me!" The auto driver turned around. "Is everything okay madam?"

They had almost reached the college; she stopped the vehicle and began to walk, away from him. There were no labs that day. She did not see Abdul at all.

She listened to the lectures, not understanding anything. That day seemed very short, she lived in some other time the whole day. Not sure what to say or what to do… frozen in time. She wrote about the summer holidays of grade 8… and a brief meeting in the tenth standard. Yes she could condense the water drops, précis writing in English was like that, and the summary was a fantastic concept for details that were only felt, unsaid. That evening, he returned late, while they were having dinner.

The next day, he did not come with her to college. She saw Abdul waiting for her outside the classroom. "Can you come with me? I want to pick up some forms from the university." She was not sure. He showed her the car. It was a white Fiat car, silver tinted glasses. He had that distant air, like someone who had a lot to say to her. Maybe she could ask him if he spoke about the kiss. So she climbed into the car. His looks were directed at the rearview mirror. Who was he searching for? She felt someone was already with them.

They drove a short distance and he slowed down saying, "Your cousin will join us." She felt very surprised… it felt like a setup.

She was utterly lonely as he entered the car. They drove in silence, the car entered a by lane, almost deserted. He spoke, "If you knew I would be coming, you would have avoided it, so I asked him to tell you a lie." So they were friends already in two days? She looked at Abdul; he did not meet her eyes. The car was parked. He spoke again, "You say you have no boyfriend, but this boy says, you guys have been necking for a while. You told him, it was your first kiss… I guess this lie is not that big a lie."

Abdul gave her his destroyed look. "He does not know that we have been in love, long before you met him. Every summer holidays you have been in my arms. I have touched you everywhere except, maybe… I have seen you without these fancy clothes. This guy thinks you belong to him."

She had counted and knew the only two summer holidays he was with her. And he had torn a dress accidentally; he made it sound like she was a willing participant. She could not get the words out of her mouth, stunned… as though passivity was consent. She had resisted, her lip was torn, and her dress was torn. Apart from one forcibly kiss and a glimpse of her chest, there was nothing. That was not love!

"So, has he read 'Jude the Obscure'? I don't think he has read even my Jackie Collins.a real suave boyfriend." Now she spoke, "No, he is not my boyfriend… you are the one I love…" There was silence. He was surprised, yet laughing, "I always knew that."

"So, if you want me to choose between the two of you, I have chosen. Can we go?" She did not wish to stay in that car. He was magnanimous; "I give few minutes to you both alone? The poor guy must know where he went wrong? He should know that." Abdul did not believe what he heard or what he saw. She was clear,

"I have nothing to say. I have nothing to say to him. Let's go!" She got down from the car. If he allowed himself to be a pawn, then he could not play the game. He followed her, jumping into the auto with her. He was jubilant.

"Why do you do such a drama when we are alone? I am dying to touch you... She felt numb. She crossed her legs. He noticed... "So excited?" She could not guess what he meant. She was merely formulating a dialogue of a scene. There was a radio in this auto obviously a live recording with long recorded applause. Endless hooting... her ears hurt.

They reached home. She went straight to her dad's room. She started without a preamble, "This guy should not stay in our house." Father nodded, "Can you give me a good reason."

She said in a steady voice, "He misbehaved with me when I was a child, kissed me in wrong places, I had a torn lip and some marks on my body, I did resist him. I could not speak about it, as I thought I was wrong for letting it happen. I was ashamed... I did not think you would believe me, better late than never, you often say that to me, so I am telling you now. I kept thinking he may not do it again, I thought I could avoid him or avoid being alone with him, I stopped going to mom's parents' house for holidays. I can't bear it if he stays in this house.

I don't want to take him to college." Dad's expression was not readable.

Her sister entered the room from somewhere, "She is not lying, and she has written it in her diary. I have read it, I can show you."

Diary never had any privacy… that is why it was created. Sindhu sounded as angry as she did when her dress was borrowed without her permission from her wardrobe. She walked away to her room, she heard voices, and screams… she did not see the end of whatever happened. He would be gone; he could not say anything about Abdul as she had taken him by surprise. She saw the half-bitten apple on her table. Brown soggy teeth marks on the cream crust. It would be sour and dry; she should not have touched it… and wasted it.

He had replaced the textbook he had borrowed from her. She heard the gate click. Mother was absent for a long time. During dinner, she looked irritated. But there was no mention of him, just the way spoons cluttered and hot aroma emanated from vessels. Father spoke about how wrong Karl Marx was about communism being a religion. He spoke about Kibbutz, it truly was a shame. He drew parallels between Mussolini and Marx. Somehow, the conversation diverted to Open University, open-book examinations and she realized for the first time that it was not a day to be forgotten easily. Kisses were cheap and she had liked one cheap kiss… that was her love letter. And even though father had torn it, she had joined the pieces and kept it. He said her eyes were like lamps…

July 18, 1995 - Saturday

Tara was sitting on one of the benches in the hospital. It was about two weeks since the last event. Pradeep came to her with a newspaper in his hands. Tara said with excitement, "I wanted to talk to you since morning where you were? Do you know that Shanthi's daughter was here to see her? It was such a moving scene. Her daughter is pregnant now, and Shanthi was quiet and happy. Though, I don't think she recognized her. Her father remarried but has no other issues, so he may help to move Shanthi to a halfway home and there if she improves more she may even go home. What is the matter with you why are you not saying anything?"

Pradeep was listless and morose. "You are happy, why should I spoil that?" Tara was concerned, "Don't be mysterious tell me what is troubling you?" Pradeep spoke in his dejected voice, "This newspaper says that a certain Miss Elena suffered acid attack yesterday and is battling for her life. They could not find the attacker, but her mother blamed one Mr. Venkatesh Pillai. He works in the same school as Elena, but preliminary investigation revealed that he was hospitalized for diarrhea four days ago and is still not discharged." Tara was aghast… "My

God, was she going to expose him after all? Did all this have to do with our anonymous letters?" Pradeep interfered, "It was my idea, remember?" Tara was indignant, "But you did it to help me. He is not even expelled from school." Pradeep said quietly, "He will be shortly, I am sure." Tara said, "Yes, it is possible that she already exposed him so her mother knows about him, even if we did protect the children, at what cost?" Pradeep was moved, it was unusual. He would never get marks for these feelings yet he had them! "It is like what you said cure anxiety it comes back as depression. Cure depression it becomes a mania. We can't stop this destruction fully. We may or may not have protected the children but another woman died trying to save them."

Tara looked down. Choke, does that spell with a C in between or not? Naïve, does that have a silent K as in Knife? Conscience, does have an S in it or only C? Humour has a U in it? Tear has A in it, but cheer has only 2 E's... Schizophrenia does that have a silent T? My mom likes Tea... that too. Three roses... not Lipton. Now, does Lipton spell as 2 Ps?

Dyslexia could be a projective test, not just Rorschach. She hated analysis... Freudian slip... A dress inside a dress... She could not get those letters with spelling mistakes out of her head...

~***~

6. mother-land

~~~~~~~~~~~~~~~~~~***~~~~~~~~~~~~~~~

"You should study not only that you become a mother when your child is born, but also that you become a child."
— Dogen (A Zen master of Pure Land Buddhism)

Another string of crackers was lit, noise flooded the air. My baby son shuddered in his sleep, the pillows that formed the fort around his sleeping form in the bed, were not tall enough to stop a fall, in case he woke up and crawled to the edge of the cot.

I disliked the crib; it looked like a cage, so he slept next to me in bed. I sat helplessly watching him sleep. He was five months old. Before he had turned three months, inside the cradle upturning it at midnight, and smiling at me when I picked him before he hit the ground, as though he knew I was more reliable than the cradle that rocked him. He had started to move backwards on his tummy from one month, like a frog. I was surprised that a sort of gravitational force worked even above the ground… making it easier to move backwards.

I had to wash his soiled napkins, sterilize his bottles, and cook dinner for the night. With this fear that he may wake up and fall, it was impossible to run the tap. The marriage ceremony in the neighborhood, causing the burn of crackers, increased the risk of him waking up.
~~~~~~~~~~~~~~~~~~

The last house help had left in a huff when I had given her Lycil oil to apply to her hair, Nizral shampoo, to be mixed with Medicare to get rid of the nits. I did not want my baby's curls to be infested with lice from her long tresses; she put her cheek to his and kissed him loudly, as though she was licking a lollypop. I thought I would at least disinfect her, she felt insulted. I was not sorry that she left, my husband was furious with me.

He was working at a project that demanded his attention for twenty-four hours, so he could not be bothered by a wife, and a wailing child, he said. I loudly announced that I would do all the work myself, but after two weeks felt weepy, when I heard any song on the radio, it did not have to be a love song. I had stopped all lullabies, I felt as though I was born in a washing machine. And once his favorite Cameron feeding bottle burnt to black crumbs, as I forgot to turn off the gas stove, and was asleep on the dining table. The gas leaked the entire night. In a panic, I had called sister Jacinta, asking her for the helper that she said needed employment. That was how I first met Rathna.

She was in her twenties, very pallid skin, huge eyes, and slender woman with a black Mangal sutra around her neck. She smiled and followed me to all the rooms, as soon as she saw the heap of the vessels in the sink, smeared with the plate powder ready to be washed, she started to wash them immediately, no questions asked.

I apologized for the dishwasher that stopped working for a while and I was housebound because of the baby. She knew about sterilizing the bottles, and every aspect of childcare. She was efficient, silent, and distant. After two days, I was slightly uncomfortable with her as she kept a distance from the baby. Whenever she saw me play with him, she retreated as though she was injured. As she was so obedient, clean, dignified, I did not want to delve into her background, lest I lose her.

My little one was moving on the blue durries for more than fifteen days, but he would tap the floor surrounding the durries incessantly, not daring to move on to the unknown ground. He did not know the coloured mattress was supported by the same floor, but he was thinking even before he knew any language, he trusted his own doubts; I found this mistrust of the ground amazing. He would support himself only on his stomach, lift both his arms and his legs, and laugh like a gymnast proudly.

I wondered about gastro-esophageal reflux that would bring up all his milk, if present, but was conspicuously absent. My tendency to run to textbooks on childcare amused Rathna. I struggled with cereal, realizing the baby was getting constipated, I boiled carrots and mixed it with formula food, I pressure cooked greens and mixed it with the formula claiming to have that flavor. My son screwed up his tiny nose and spat it all at me.

I tried all the formula foods available in the market, he showed uniform dislike. He looked at me in the eye, made an obnoxious face, wondering why I was so stupid as to not understand. I lost my appetite, worrying over all the nutrients he would be deprived of in crucial months of growth.

Rathna saw me tempt Jeeva for days, to tread on the unknown ground, then one fine day she simply lifted him and left him on the floor. He was elated by the firmness beneath his body and started moving forward at top speed on his tummy, encountered several interesting objects on his expedition, checked out many with his drooling mouth. He greeted me cheerfully babbling as though now that he knew to reach me, he was self-reliant. She knew that the mother had to make some decisions for the baby, he could not think, he only feared.

I felt truly grateful that she knew to do this, she definitely had loved some baby, and I decided not to ask as I sensed an invisible shell around her that may break if I asked her personal questions. I had encountered a cold wall over some inane queries and decided to maintain a professional silence.

I started to look down whenever I walked around the house, scared that I may step on him. I had recollections of horror films like Bhaktha Kumbara (Devoted Potter) - A movie where a veteran actor, a potter in the film, in his devotion to the lord, steps on his baby son crushing him. I kept dashing my head with taller objects, as I was avoiding the angel sprawled on the floor.

Rathna slowly advised me one day about the native preparation of nine dals, to be sprouted and dried in the sun, mixed with Jaggery and milk to be fed to babies. I found a packet in some shop and walked home victorious. But my son treated this with equal disdain, I was in tears.

Finally, I mashed cooked rice with dhal mixed it with ghee and salt, dropped all the rubber spoons, in my one finger fed him; he ate a reasonable amount and fell asleep satiated. I could not sterilize my hands, so I just used my finger sparingly, petrified of transferring some infection to him.

But Rathna was a silent witness to all my travails. She was a friend of the mother that I was learning to be, but she did not bond with my baby. She never once picked him, nor interested to pet him. She read papers, she was educated. Jeeva had stood up holding on to every piece of furniture he could find around, it was something new every day. I was learning or unlearning what meaning the physical world had assumed in my eyes before. Like big bang theory, the universe was just eight months old for me…!

As he learnt to stand up on his own and I was sure it was not a strain on his spine, we learnt this new game of him standing on my feet and I would walk around the house holding his palms in mine and his little feet on my feet. It gave him a sort of practice walk before he actually walked. My feet enjoyed his weight on them like a massage. So, both pairs of happy feet made this cat-kitten walk a favorite between us.

Once when both I and Jeeva were down with a fever, Rathna cooked. My husband was not in town and I could not calm the baby. I asked her to carry the baby, she refused. I was completely irritated I asked her, "What is your anger towards an innocent baby? Why are you so indifferent to him?" It was three months since she worked for me. I felt I had a right to know. Or just that I was visibly vulnerable maybe she would not resent opening up at this juncture.

She said, "Truth is not happiness." I persisted "I want to know." She spoke for the first time. She was working in the orphanage attached to the church in which Sister Jacinta stayed. She was five months pregnant when she went there.

"I am a widow. I was married to a wealthy orphan with greedy relatives. My father was an alcoholic, as I was pretty; my marriage did not cost him a rupee. I tried to extricate my husband from his greedy relatives, but he met with an accident and died when I was pregnant, so I became helpless. Afraid for my life and that of the unborn child I sought asylum in the church. The nuns asked me to work in the orphanage; I loved taking care of babies." Her voice was shaking; there was tenderness in the tone, akin to what she expressed towards my inefficiency at times.

"They asked me how I was going to rear my child without support, I had none. Over several weeks I saw couples coming to adopt babies. They were rich, came in cars. The nuns kept telling me that if I really wanted to be a good mother, I could give up my baby in adoption. Then the baby would have all that I can never give him, I was confused. I was so attached to the babies in the orphanage, the most stubborn, with the most difficult temperament, played with me. When they left the place with a mother, I felt a loss. But after several sessions with the head of the institution, I signed an agreement to give up my baby in adoption."

She was weeping. "When my son was born, I fell in love with him, I did not want to part from him. It was a normal delivery; I took my son on the fourth day and left the orphanage. But I was unable to look after my child and myself in the village. I fell sick with a fever. My son had also contracted fever, so after one week I went back to the orphanage."

"The nuns took me back, but my son slept in one of the cradles of the orphanage. I breastfed many babies that needed breast milk to survive, some rejected the cow's milk. My son drank cow's milk so he did not need mine. But late at nights I would creep into his cradle and try to feed him. His right ear was folded, he had a mole on his right hand, I can identify anywhere. I was sent to the tailoring section of the institution, for a few days. I had developed diarrhea, vomiting. I was too weak to breastfeed. I cut clothes, for a week, but went to the orphanage at night. The pain of engorged milk was unbearable, so I went. They did not allow me to visit the floor where my son's cradle was placed. I felt frantic after fifteen days of this, I asked the nuns for my son, but I had signed the papers, the second time when I had returned. He was gone."

"My milk dried up. I could not stay in that orphanage, I could not hear a baby cry, I felt it was my child calling me. I was given medicines, I felt stiff and vacant. I don't blame them, I signed up. I wanted him to have it all, a house, wealth, education everything that I could not give him. But I feel like seeing him… that is all. Just know where he is, who his mother is now… that is all. From two years I go to all those houses where there are small children. I thought your child was two years old, I did not know he was so tiny. I am now a good mother; I can only love my son. I fed all other babies in the orphanage when he was there, but once he was gone, I lost it. Am I a good mother?" She asked that question to herself, she did not even care for my answer.

"Was I disloyal for feeding others? Maybe, it would have been better if I died, on the roads with him on my lap. So many women beg with small babies in tow, why I did not? I studied up to the tenth standard in my village, did not write tenth exams, because my father stole my gold earrings to purchase his drinks, and tied me up in a chair, as he did not want trouble. Now I don't know why I gave him up. I am jealous of every mother, but I understand your fears… I can't bear to even look at your baby. My son was sixty days old when he was sent away."

I was silent all through this narration, but now I tried, "Some adoptive parents tell the child, some children look for the mother. Your son might come searching for you someday."

She was horrified, "No, no! He should never know. I can't face him, I failed him. I just want to see him as a third person, I am a third person, I want to see him happy. I want a confirmation that what I did was right, giving him up was right for him, I wanted him to be a police inspector."

She thought for a while, "I had refused out of country adoption, I said only in India he should grow. Then at least accidentally I may meet him, or else I will never see him. They would have done that surely. Is it not?"

"Of course!" I was not prepared for this plea. She went to the kitchen to fetch milk. I held my son on my lap. So, what was a good mother? How to sacrifice a love that was such an instinct for his social survival, the survival of the fittest? How did she live with such anguish? Those hopes of seeing her son, why can't the nuns tell her where her son was? Then, I thought of a two years old toddler in another woman's lap, kissing her, could this mother of sixty days bear it? What was this loyalty, what was this possessiveness, what was this feeling? She was clearly a mother even before the birth of her son; she cared for so many babies in the orphanage.

I thought of every two or three years old little girl engaged in hugging a Barbie or Dora, bathing her, grooming her… every little girl was a born mother. And the miniature houses built by every little child in pillows between sofa sets, human was a family animal.
Losing that which belonged to her and feeling responsible for that loss, like cutting off her own nose.

She was vulnerable and they exploited her vulnerability, stripping the only reason that kept her alive for all other orphans in the orphanage. This was worse than Mother India of Nargis, a film I had watched as a child and my loud sobs at appropriate scenes of loss had disturbed the entire theatre, now I had to remind myself that I was dealing with reality.

Was there a provision in the law for a biological mother to change her mind about adoption? Postpartum psychosis or depression may have messed up her decision-making capacity, other than brainwashing by those who gained by such a decision, I had to consult textbooks on laws of adoption. Limitation period before a law can be revoked, hence a contract can be cancelled, but where was her son?

I recollected the quiet confidence with which she had placed my son on the bare ground. He just had to learn to trust the ground, he had to grow. Both of us slept through the night. When I woke up the next morning, I saw that the door was ajar. She had left all the clothes I had given her in a neat bundle; there was a letter on top of it. She had torn a paper from my diary.

"Sister forgive me. After knowing what a bad mother I was in giving up my own child, I don't think you will keep me. Before you send me away, I myself want to leave with dignity. You are a very kind woman; I could not help confiding in you. This diary in which you have written all the lullabies in your mother-tongue is so beautiful; I have taken it with me. I have not taken anything else from your house. Sister, I want you to know that you are a very good mother, be confident. Don't ever lose your son as I did. -Rathna."

I was speechless. I wish she had that conviction and fought for her child in those days that were crucial. Maybe if she trusted me to be kind, she should have known that I would have tried to find her son. My intuition that I would lose her if I extracted the truth out of her had come true. I should have given her time to disclose at her own pace. I had forced a confession, I was filled with remorse.

I called sister Jacinta who did not know Rathna's destination either. I knew Rathna was depressed, hence was a child searching for a parent, how could she handle this second orphan hood bestowed on her by the loss of her child? Insecure childhood shaping resilient brave hearts to fall as parents... how difficult it was to return what one never received from the universe and only knew in dreams? To be forced to transcend biology was inhuman. Every amoeba wanted to become two amoebae; it was a code in every cell.

I recalled a cat that was a visitor to my house a few years ago. She was perhaps domesticated by another family, she would come in mewing till I put milk in a bowl, I liked her since she never drank milk without me serving it to her. She would mew before she entered a room as if asking permission. She made it clear that she was just a visitor and never stayed overnight.

I noticed one day that her abdomen was swollen and she meowed even after drinking milk and later curled up in one of my wooden cupboards containing old curtains and kurtas. I suspected she wanted to have her kittens in that cupboard. She did, five little adorable kittens were born, at some hour in the night. She did not show me the kittens; she would emerge out of the cupboard only to drink milk. I slept in the bedroom next to hers.

One of those nights I heard loud meows and a scuffle, it was raining outside, I switched on the lights in her room, and the window was open because of strong gusts of wind. The floor below the window was wet with rain, a huge Tom cat emerged from the cupboard, and his face was carrying scratches of blood. He looked menacing and jumped out of the window. I was worried for the cat who had delivered two days ago, as the cupboard was half-opened I saw her lift her head and bend over the kittens. I presumed she was alright and left the room securing the door and windows. Next day I realized that the male cat had slit the throats of all the kittens as the mother was not in heat, refused to copulate with him.

She was an animal ruled by biology; she would refuse rape and could not predict the consequence of losing her kittens. She had carried the dead kittens out of the cupboard in her jaws. Meowed at my feet pathetically, I felt quite distraught. She did not come for several months afterwards; I guess post-traumatic stress disorder could affect animals too. Animal world was harsh and cruel dictated by instincts only. It was human to understand the animal. It was human to not violate the rights of another. The helplessness I felt then was similar…

I understood hormones; I had to forgive testosterone also… if I was empathizing with progesterone. I read the bible again. Christ saying that the Kingdom of God is within us (Luke 17:21). I read law, our law was reformative, it let a hundred criminals escape but would not punish one innocent person. She had three years to revoke her decision. After that, it was the decision of the adoptive mother.

She was blaming herself for that decision made in learnt helplessness, for being brainwashed to believe that she had to sacrifice her biological instinct of a mother to be a good mother! Interference of a perverted brain in the matters of the heart masked as extra virtue. Her virtue was exploited… I shed some useless tears for the splendid mother I had experienced like a gift. She had chosen to bond only with me, like a loyal child. She had left fearing my judgment, it was premature disclosure. She should have realized that it was not her fault and then disclosed. I should have waited.

Some lonely nights, when there is no moon but a star shines in the sky like a precious stone, I think of her. I think of her stoic silence of three months. I wonder where she is, whether she is still searching for her son in his mother-land.

~***~

Gandhari

She blinded her eyes
She did not see her husband
Who could not see her
She never saw the world
Her husband did not see
So believed the world
The world could only see
What it wanted to see…

7. a stage of reactions

~~~~~~~~~~~~~~~~~~***~~~~~~~~~~~~~~~

Sudha, felt as though she was not herself any more, as though something very vital had ceased to be. It was angst… there were minutes, sometimes hours that were sort of lost as she could not find those times. She looked at the clock that made the same revolutions every day and though a witness to the lost time, could not show her how it had passed. Whenever she was alone, she was frightened… of whom? No idea… of what? Nothing visible. She had frightening nightmares of being seminude in a house full of strangers. She saw a bedspread with blood spots, woke up drenched with sweat. She had begun to write poems… to make sense of the images.

At times trying to find a mythical character who may have felt what she felt. Or to be accurate the opposite of what she felt. She knew she was in denial, accepting distress felt like a defeat. No one was honest. So, she tried to cheat herself to laugh when she felt like being at the bottom of a well. No one heard her cry. It was not respectable emotion that could be spoken about. It was 'unlove'. It was not chastity, an unopened flower that was hidden in anticipatory silence. It was not passion that made others envy, it was not the urge of lovers to unite at least in death… ferocious adulterous love that did not care about being pelted stones at. Even disrespectable love had the respectability of being at least love. This was
~~~~~~~~~~~~~~~~~~

not that. She was unable to accept her body that had betrayed her in pain, not in pleasure.

She thought of women who had loved like Heloise. "Let me be your whore," she said. But Abelard married her and then they castrated him. Penelope turned down 108 suitors as she waited for 20 years for Odysseus. Why then she wasn't capable of that lofty emotion? Pretending was tiresome.

One evening Sudha accompanied her father and mother to watch a play on the epic of Draupadi, an important character in Mahabharata, rendered in folk style by a local theatre group. Draupadi is the wife and queen of Pandavas , five in number. The one woman who was legitimately polyandrous. As she entered the auditorium, she heard a female voice singing on the stage. It was so beautifully honest, rustic, and passionate. Sudha was struck; such power dripped from that voice, anger could be melodious?!

This voice was like fire, like smoldering coals, like the hot lava of a volcano. The honesty of that voice was nude, shameless, free, impatient, insistent, reflecting the soul of a gipsy, who did not even want to belong. The voice was pulsating with a life, an emotion which was beyond the song or the tune. There was a raw passion, anger, it was primitive, completely lacking inhibition. It was like a wild forest fire, inherently destructive, deeply disturbing.

Sudha was sweating with emotion; she did not want that voice to stop. There was a secret vein deep inside her, which was engorged with this voice, frightening her with unseen possibilities of her unleashed anger. The woman who was singing was a veteran, a descendant of a famous clan of folk theatre. She was the creative head of the theatre group called 'Reaction'. It dealt with plays of epics, periods, treated in a contemporary style. That was the 'in' thing, fusion they called it. Sudha could not appreciate twisting the story to suit a convenient end. Just that definition of convenient had changed in these plays.

Here every woman was a reactionary; she was condemned to be different, with the smallest of provocation. Sudha, being a student of life sciences knew that homeostasis was apparently precarious, but once achieved is resistant to the atmosphere. So showing women who did not even try to compromise, rebelled from the word go, seemed contrived. Like being born to commit suicide, it appeared to be bourgeoisie, so she avoided such plays. Besides, it had the paradoxical effect of making her conform vehemently for days afterwards.

This play was indeed different both in the rendition and in the content; it did focus on Krishna as a brother to Draupadi and Subhadra. The soul twin-ship of a polygamous Krishna with a polyandrous Draupadi was interesting. The non-possessiveness of Krishna's eroticism liberates him, elevates him to divinity, whereas it victimizes Draupadi, humiliating her. She is pawned in a game, as none of her husbands are possessive of her, yet treats her as a possession; she is disrobed in public as every man wants his carnal pleasure from her because she already has multiple partners. Whereas Krishna chooses to be polygamous, Draupadi accommodates polyandry imposed on her by a mother-in-law.

A beautiful fire child, she had never known a real mother, so was powerless before maternal authority, not knowing the subtle difference between a mother and mother-in-law. Mother-in-law only mothered the erotic object of her son. That was not how her own mother would have nurtured her. Kunthi, a matriarch united her sons and stepsons born to multiple Gods. She attempted the repetition of united brotherhood through sharing the pleasures of one flesh. That flesh was one woman; no one asked her what her wish was. Or was it mother –in law politics, Kunthi did not want Draupadi to have a moral authority over a mother in law , who had sons from different Gods ? Krishna courted every woman, never once eroticized Draupadi. Was he a puritan ?

She compromised to live with her husbands after the public ignominy. Her undone hair, like her undone clothes, looked like compliance, not at all boasting of rebellion. There really was no retribution. No matter how many different versions of the original were dramatized, a queen being stripped in front of her husbands for the sport was chillingly obscene, humiliating for any woman who watched. That scene had no resolution, not in the eighteen chapters of war, or in the bloodshed soaking her tresses. At least now, there was a law forbidding the outrage of modesty of women.

Like injury was the start of all physical love between man and woman, nudity and its irreversible association with shame was also gender-specific. A woman could not rape a man, to hell with Freud's penis envy, thought Sudha.

Choreography and stagecraft were brilliant, the voice haunted. It was as though a thorn was sprouting from the soft petals of a blood-red rose; as though a thousand scorpions were stinging simultaneously, as though her bones were being powdered, the sound of a conch heralding an unknown battle, flooding of the senses. That voice could emote the recklessness which assaulted Sudha, that wild impulse to fall off a cliff, it was commanding, like the voice of a tribal goddess.

Sudha decided to work with this lady Samprada and her theatre group, so she went backstage with her dad as he knew her. Most of her decisions were instantaneous, after prolonged periods of inaction; she just 'knew' when she felt like doing something. It had to be when all of her wanted it, without a doubt.

The lady was petite, her eyes gleamed, and she looked coarse. So, the ferocious voice, distinctly feminine, had a shrewd, macho face. Samprada was graceful, courteous, warmly welcomed Sudha to join her group and meet them at her office located in a college auditorium. Sudha was excited with this venture, for drama enticed her. The body or the person simply did not exist for Sudha, she was relating to that voice of passion. That voice had a presence of its own; it was beyond the body that housed her.

When she entered college as per the instruction, it was evening, some students whose hobby was ham, a wireless messaging, were around. They were connecting with signals in distress. But some distress was voiceless. So voicing distress was an art, not at all easy. Here it had Morse code, a series of dots, composed a language.

Like a series of holes of Braille, which could be touched, here series of dots could be heard, even across a tempestuous ocean to rescue an explorer who was homeless. All language stemmed from that original universal language 'cry'. This distressing language was perforated, like the flowerpot. To make distress understandable was so difficult; sometimes it was easier to sing. Sudha sighed; there was a stage in the central open space, surrounded by college classrooms. The rains had wet the sands in that open space, some stray letters or notes were sticking to the wet sands.

Leaves were soggy and were floating on the waters of shallow pools formed in the cement ground. Sudha made a small paper boat, in one of the pages and let it float in the waters. Another young man was loitering around, waiting. Sudha self-consciously stopped her activity and found a place to sit and read. Slowly some men arrived, it was a heterogeneous group of various ages, two more women were present, and they were much older.

Samprada arrived with an older man, head full of grey hair; there was a companionship about them as it clearly distanced others. Most of the men worked for some factories, were married with children, but they did theatre to escape the mundane, to recreate fantasy. They were curious about her; she did introduce herself. One young man with a pleasant face was being mischievous and constantly drawing attention. So he belonged to the stage, he had an insatiable need for attention. Samprada pampered his childish games, with dramatic disciplining actually chasing him with a stick, the others laughing and taking sides. There were several rounds of laughter, some good-natured fooling around. They did not treat her like an outsider, they constantly invited her to tease them, and they laughed at themselves, treating her with gentleness. It was endearing.

They all appeared to be misfits in their respective areas of work, wanting to be somebody else; feeling trapped by any identity imposed on them by the cogwheel of the social machinery that constantly put them in a known slot. They thought they belonged on stage, Sudha differed there.

She felt she was a misfit to live or love, she fitted into work, most forms of it, any form of it, reducing her to a fluid always in need of a container. She preferred a routine, with just one intimate hour. Total impersonal clock and uniforms of measured small talk, strict boundaries of 'Never Personal'… neither take it as personal nor offer the personal was suffocating, like a huge prison. The world was like this endless prison. Obviously, she could not find herself; she tried to normalize this pathology.

The young man was Gopi; he worked as a clerk in Samprada's office. The older man was the manager of that troupe. His name was Sachidanand, he was eager to befriend Sudha. As she talked to him she became aware of Samprada's attention which was following their talk, annoyed. So it was definitely more than platonic love that Samprada felt for this man. That insecurity was not the righteous indignation of a wife, but the jealous watch of the other woman.

Women in love were so vulnerable, no matter how successful they were, no matter how many times they had felt that before. An invisible wall existed between Sudha and Samprada from then onwards; Samprada disliked that air of aristocracy, inherent conformity of so-called good upbringing, emanating from Sudha. That nonconformist wrath of Samprada which Sudha admired disapproved and mistrusted this admiration. A woman born to a polygamous marriage of a theatre veteran of yesteryears, who saw her parents cry in the guise of king and queen, reared in the chaos, lawlessness of a creative jungle of talents of a hoard of step-siblings, scorned Sudha's propriety. Inner gentleness of a well-bred convent child, singing Christmas carols, wearing strawberry gloss, irritated the tribal goddess, who perceived all self-control as hypocrisy.

Though, her lover Sachidanand seemed to be a paragon of sophisticated hypocrisy. Why did women dislike the very same qualities in another woman, but worshipped them in a man? Sudha was hurt by this silent intolerance. The men, young and old were affected by her, sensing some inner sadness of her spirit, pampered her with attention. Unlike Samprada they did not consider her to be a spoilt brat. But Samprada was incredibly talented, she danced like a Yakshagana artist, dramatic exaggeration of movements, there was no subtlety. It was as though the cognitive rhythm of the music was attempting to dance, her dance lacked the vivacity and the grace of her voice. Any musical instrument would be ashamed to hear the calibre of her voice, which could hammer like a drum, lilt like a violin, whistle like a flute, twang like a veena. She did not need the body as an instrument.

Her humor was contrived, hysterical. Anger was her element, like fire, it was purifying. She raged, thundered, reinvented anger, making it natural, effortless, and vaguely intimate. This anger was royal, not stealthy or deceptive like a serpent; it was open like the roar of a lioness. Anger implied ownership, it was missing in her depiction of love, that seemed distant. That loneliness inarticulately eating every artist was hers too. Sudha watched Samprada enact a folk dance, training the actors. Samprada hesitantly called Sudha, who joined in gracefully. Collective dance was therapeutic.

Sudha went to her theatre meetings regularly. They managed to keep her smiling for their audience. She found it difficult to control her emotions at times when Samprada burst into one of her songs of love, hate, betrayal. The high pitch of her fearless voice ringing with pathos and anger alternately at times was too much to bear. The actors were incessantly curious about her person, dropping personal questions in a non-obtrusive style. Sudha's desire to be a stranger without a definite or distinct individuality, absorbing the voice of the tribal goddess was becoming impossible. With every passing day she revealed vital aspects of her emotional existence to one member or the other unwillingly. As long as they all did not conduct a collective conference behind her they would not be able to put together the jigsaw puzzle. She wanted to lose herself. Though it frightened her, annihilation was welcome. Other option was to return to that damaged sheets of cells, it spelt definite pain.

The women were smoking, getting drunk over their lovers and weeping for the broken hearts of their fathers and mothers. The complete lack of discipline, near-total flouting of conventions, soaked that atmosphere. Sudha was bewildered by this tribe of gypsies; she did not belong here. These people seemed more honest and genuinely warm, that much she had to concede.

Most of the members shared a long romantic history with other members. Now those tangles had matured into a sexless deep familiarity with one another. This excited curiosity about her would stay till she got romantically entangled with one member then the others would feel as though they all would get their turns in time to romance with her, a sort of game-like musical chair. Sudha consciously decided to remain an outsider to this circle or clique. She was beginning to feel like an alien everywhere. Since no one understood her anyways, she was being herself everywhere. The need to erect defenses, hiding behind masks was unnecessary as her real self could not be under siege by individuals who did not understand anything about her.

She was safely misunderstood as a brat, a hoax, broken-hearted waif, adopted (or even more romantic, illegitimate) daughter of a rich man. *They thought her humility to be a secret justified inferiority.* In short, a poor little rich girl. Some believed that she was recovering from a serious case of 'love failure'. Why else would a girl like her, not even have a boyfriend? Just as she let her colleagues think her social life was saturated with several admirers who were all drunk, she let actors believe that she was indeed a lovesick waif, uncared wayward child. No single identity could explain all of her to her own self so she let each person conjure whatever picture suited his whim and fancy and caprice.

She was lonely in this group as it was united in making money in the shortest possible time. Sudha felt broken inside and needed the mythical characters of the epics who were resurrected, or séance on stage by Samprada. So she came to that college day after day, forlorn and expecting. She was searching for the childhood crowns of silver foils, veils designed from her mother's sexy lingerie (the only erotic gift from her father picked by him during his trips abroad) in those dusty government college empty corridors, dotted by the ham signals, and the confident fearless ancient melody of the witch. The abandon of the wilderness of the jungles nestled in the folk songs, strangely reminding her of the home she knew in the lap of the Malnad hills with the shroud of the simplicity of a village.

Sudha came for those songs and the burning rage of innumerable characters of Ramayan, Mahabharath who danced under Samprada's spell, wielded by her voice. Anger was so closely interwoven with love for centuries by women, somehow only names changed over the years, the stories did not change. Marriage as a system exploited some like Gandhari (Was married off to Dhritharashtra a blind prince, without her knowledge. She blind folded herself in protest and the world hailed her as virtuous!) and Draupadi. Not being married was why Shakunthala and Amba felt betrayed. Amba, Ambika, Ambalika were the three daughters of a king during their swayamvar (choose your groom) Bhishma interfered, defeating all the suitors. But Amba was in love with Salwa, so she refused to wed Bhishma's step brothers. But Salwa refused Amba; she was the conquest of a rival. She symbolized a humiliating defeat. Bhishma refused to marry Amba, as he had taken a vow to be celibate. Amba finally chose to self-immolate and reincarnate as a transgender. Denouncing sexuality meant amputating a faculty, like deliberate self-harm it spelt ultimate cowardice. *'I will harm myself, I won't let you harm me...'* that stance bestowed him with a clear conscience, fulfilling his objective, how stupid! Besides amputation made phantoms out of what was once normal and pain more by its absence.

Maybe love was mere imagination, just a longing, memory of one moment, a promise which may not be kept at all. Those brief series of involuntary contractions of one fleshy hole deep inside her when all other sensations merge into one feeling of thoughtless ecstasy, was that love? Most men lived for that one moment, it seemed. But why did she think it could be more than that? Why was she so hurt by this discovery, that love was a mere sensation of a bodily organ? A voluntary stimulus triggering a set of involuntary muscular contractions, coded to be interpreted as pleasant to merely ensure the continuation of species.

They will be simply changing the names, it will always be the same story, permutations and combinations of 'Catch *me if you can', 'If you want to run I want to hold you, then when you cling I want to dump you', 'if you are not possessive, I will suspect your fidelity. If you are possessive, I won't belong to you', 'if your intellect is aware, I will look for innocence, if you are innocent then I will mess with it till you become aware of all my traps, perils', 'if you do you are damned, if you don't you are damned, and you can't die…'* Sudha was so tired of all these games, no one was genuine except for their petty needs of social prominence, a better car, a posh house, one more degree, one more drink, one more fuck. She had not abandoned her Gods, they had abandoned the earth. There were no flowers growing on the disturbed earth.

The amorous advances of two men, in the theatre group, Gopi and Rakshith, began in a subtle way. She was there to affirm a role. She needed to rehearse that on stage so that she could discharge it in life. It was serious, a sort of resolution, catharsis, a secret therapy. She had to experience that anger, which she was afraid of, see how far she could go about it in a civilized route. To be distracted in that mission by these two men was exasperating. Samprada was planning to stage two of her plays in the national theatre festival of Jaipur so rehearsals were scheduled regularly.

The play based on the epic, Mahabharath, and Ramayan had the theme of 'Estrangement'. It depicted Sumithra, Lakhshman's wife who stays alone in Ayodhya waiting for him, Madri a beautiful wife of Pandu doing sati for sleeping with a husband who dies due to a medical ailment which had forbidden him from indulging in sex, Shakunthala living alone with her illegitimate child Bharath, as her lover is amnesic about his affair, Amba a princess who commits suicide to avenge being conquered like an immovable asset by Bhishma separating her from her lover Salwa, and is reincarnated as a eunuch to kill Bhishma.

Sudha had to play the role of Amba, Gopi was Salwa and Rakshith was Bhishma. The Swayamvara (choose a husband, a rare privilege of princesses) ceremony of the three princesses Amba, Ambika and Ambalika began the scene. But before the eldest princess chooses to tie the knot with her lover, a war breaks out where Bhishma, a celibate king fights all the attendant princes of the Swayamvara and captures the princesses, against their will and takes them to his capital Hasthinapura to wed his stepbrothers. Amba revolts goes to Bhishma and requests to be set free as she loves Salwa and can't marry another man. Bhishma though a celibate is portrayed as a patriarch known for his impeccable sense of justice. As a noble son, he sacrificed his erotic manhood for a father's second marriage to a fisherwoman. She demanded that her children alone should succeed the throne; hence her stepson should not marry and reproduce. Bhishma was saved from being killed by his mother Ganga, by a father, who loses her for his son. So, it is a sacrifice of the father returned by the son.

Bhishma apologetically set Amba free. Amba goes to her lover Salwa wanting to solemnize their love into a marriage, but he refuses. Now she is only a reminder of his failure to defeat Bhishma. She is a territory of the enemy, Bhishma's flag of victory. Amba pleads for her love, affirming that she is a person, not a territory to be conquered, or possessed against her will. It is a violation of her human rights, to be pawned in a game or sold in a market or lost in a war. But she is up against a system, a whole orthodox pattern of thinking, patriarchy, monarchy. She is so pained by this rejection that she goes back to Bhishma and pleads with him to marry her, though she is aware of his famous vow to be a celibate. To be conquered by a man who does not even desire her, has no plans of marrying her enrages her. Here the manhood of patriarchy is split in half.

The Chithra Veerya and Vichithraveerya, the stepbrothers of Bhishma are mere seminal vesicles to continue the clan, erotic elements. Bhishma is the valorous king the aggressive element. On the flip side, he is a pimp, or a marriage broker or a hierophant to bless marriage a man whose potency is exhibited on battleground only. A victim of virtue, a condemned angel whose release by an enlightened mother was thwarted by an ignorant father.

A man who can't express Eros is hailed as a great warrior. A woman reflects his elements because he obstructs her love, she fights him. But first she renounces her sexuality as a woman; as the man who can claim that aspect no longer desires her, she fights Bhishma as a Eunuch. So the role definition of a woman was so stringent, aggression was anathema for her. Even before she felt the anger she had to be burnt alive, become a flame and ash. And from the ashes would rise a eunuch.

Only a man had the right to refuse sex and not be called a eunuch but glorified as a celibate. A woman could not refuse sex and be hailed as a celibate, but suffer the tags of frigidity or eunuch. And though she had never really said the words *'Will you marry me?'* to any man earnestly, would never ask that of a man, the thought of wanting to marry a man and be refused was humiliating.

The scene of swayamvara where the princesses enter, Sudha had to raise the veil hiding her face, each time she did that some older actor would hoot and whistle, making her blush genuinely. Rakshith was a graduate of the National School of Drama, but his physical attributes made him the most unsuitable actor for the role of Bhishma. He was fair, tall and ugly. He was actually a comedian at heart. Sudha knew by observation to be a comedian required superior intelligence, it was not easy. But he was wasted in that play, his real talent was untapped.

Sudha despised him because he understood her love of comedy, tried to access the pathos underlying her jokes, a clever ploy to extract intimate confidences. Because she tried to make her own pain appear foolish. She sensed in him a man who never laughed at himself, but made others laugh at things, events and also at themselves. Most of it was of him taking the most ridiculous aspect of a person damn seriously. His type of joking was cruel, sadistic. To defame another's sense of integrity, rotten tomatoes camouflaged as apple cherries, a pair of stinking slippers clothed in royal silk, pretending to be funny tickles or mere cartoons.

The laughter was gone from his chest, he was cold and shrewd. Gopi, on the other hand, made others laugh at him, hoping to endear himself to others, he was vulnerable to appreciation. Rakshith had oodles of arrogant self-assurance; appreciation did not affect him at all. Why did all the audience sympathize with Jerry more than Tom? Because Jerry was smaller? Gopi had the advantage a truly stupid person had in playing a fool, people trusted him to be harmless. So this unspoken competition between Gopi the cynosure of Samprada's eyes and Rakshith a trained clever actor with finely honed skills for superiority in the group, on the stage, improved the general performance of the group.

But from the minute Sudha had joined that group there was a change in Gopi, half of his pranks and antics were meant to draw her attention. He was so interested in her, it was impossible to ignore him, yet to her, he seemed very immature. She knew he was trapped in some stage of childhood; he had probably taken a responsibility a child should not have, had not lived the innocence of childhood, hence kept on reliving it the moment someone patted him. The more he laughed she saw several shades of pain, inferiority, a sort of orphan hood begging for adoption.

Samprada had responded to that plea, she had sort of adopted him, pampered him, and liked his worship of her. Sudha tried not to be intense in her portrayal of Amba. That emotion of a woman in love begging a man to love her, unashamedly on her knees was an act she abhorred in real life. To risk all of her self - respect, drop all her defenses, and beg was so humiliating and unthinkable. This act violated her.

But Gopi disliked her begging equally, he hated himself for refusing, he did not enjoy that scene at all, he detested a woman to be at his mercy. This feeling of discomfort which he communicated so effectively moved Sudha, so she respected him. He diluted the effect of those dialogues, her action of falling on her knees, by himself falling on the ground after she completed the act, making her laugh, and his humor was so refreshingly kind. Nevertheless, whenever she begged, she was unpleasantly reminded of a similar instance. It caused her eyes to go wet, by humiliation.

But her act with Bhishma enraged her, the tirade of words, how dare he capture her, how dare he order her to marry his brother? What sort of justice dictated the war on an enemy when he was planning a marriage of his daughters? What sort of war whose trophy was women prisoners for sexual pleasure, what sort of a marriage conducted due to defeat of the bride to protect herself from the tyrant? A single brave princess fighting the system, for losing a love which was never love. How tragic! What sort of lover, who treated his love as mere property, a territory, once conquered a symbol of his defeat? So when men could not view love as an equal partnership, but made a woman a passive prize to be won to prove their military feat, what were her options?

The war between two men, the woman as the trophy was as inhuman as the sport of dice between men with the woman as the object of the gamble. A woman flouting the conventions suffered even more than the woman who complied. Why burn for a Salwa who was not a lover at all? Why kill Bhishma who was not a man at all? But what else she could have done, what was left of being a woman? When any relationship with a man becomes a political game of power, why be a woman?

There was no salvation in the drama, death of Amba did not resolve the issue, and it depressed Sudha, who was grappling with that issue. The experience of womanhood even before it began had hurt Sudha, so this drama glorified that self-pity, she hated it. Somehow insane vulnerability in an attractive young woman was desirable to men, reminding them of their manhood, their power over a woman. So Bhishma (Rakshith) was upset by her fury which was choking her. He tried all his charm to soften her after the rehearsal. To fight this game of love and loss, on stage was bad enough, so to suffer that fight between the two young men for her attention off the stage depleted her.

Every word, gesture, of camaraderie by her, was being misinterpreted as a romantic inclination towards one of them when she cared for neither. She liked Gopi as a friend that is all; in a situation she would trust him to be a gentleman. But she was weary of the Rakshiths of the world who used their heads in matters of the heart, like military generals to settle a score.

They credited a woman with very little brain, sure of their capacity to manipulate her hidden nerves and veins. Just because she was a pretty young woman she had to put up with being pursued everywhere, anywhere she went. She was fed up of saying 'no' when she needed love, but no one man attracted her, she attracted everyone. She had no intention of being a femme fatale but was treated like one. She often longed for a world, a tiny one where she could be treated as a person, a human being and not as a female body.

Samprada cleverly observed the dynamics but chose to subtly encourage it. Sudha had a habit of depending on gentle father figures, and in that group, that role belonged to Sachidaanand. And Samprada wanted Sudha to be quickly linked to a young man. She did not trust Sudha's innocent attachment to the older man seeking protection from unwanted sexual attention. In this world of uninhibited self-expression, morality had a single definition of gratification of the senses.

Sachidanand, was an absent woman's husband, so a world where swapping spouses were permitted why trust a single attractive woman? Sudha respected the monogamy a marriage was supposed to uphold. Sachidanand was a married man though not to Samprada. Why should Gopi enjoy the status of an adopted son by her, but Sudha not be the favorite daughter of Sachidaanand? Samprada had very little experience of the passionate morality which Sudha was immensely capable of. She desperately wanted to forget herself, be amidst people, but be treated as a person; she was tired of this sexual harassment. Unfortunately, in any group until she got linked to one man, all other men tried for her, and it felt like multiple assaults.

As long as she was single, they presumed she was available, it persecuted her, and she wanted her sexuality to be left alone.

The second play was meant for children, it was also a folk tale of a princess rendered in a folk style. A princess by name Damayanthi is happy in a kingdom of agro-economy, amidst nature. But famine visits her land and she learns that there is a gem which brings rain to the arid land. But she needs to take a pilgrimage to a distant land and undergo a rigorous penance to procure the gem, which she does. But on her way back home some demons steal her gem. She is so distressed by the loss of the precious gem that she dances in grief before a goddess who had bestowed her gem and kills herself. A prince of that land falls in love with the princess in eternal sleep. He is told by the goddess to retrieve the gem of the princess from the demons only that can resurrect her. So he hunts down the demons, restores the gem and marries her. In this play, Gopi was the prince, she was the princess.

This gem which caused showers what was it, love, innocence, or purity? Somehow Sudha's emotions responded to losses, with acute grief, there was a selective non-responsiveness towards happy events. After all the destruction of the fire, what was the role of the rain? Ashes dry or wet, were remains of ruin nothing resurrected it, once a gem was lost, it was lost forever. No prince wanted to rescue her, a love she could not procure in life, how to procure it in sleep? She wanted rebirth as someone else, no resurrection. She was tired of this identity. She hated the rain; those drops of water falling made her ache for a different season. Thunder spoke of the battle of the clouds; she wanted to tie a farewell message to the feet of a gentle dove to quieting the warring clouds. Not even rain was worth fighting for...

There was a huge green cloth tree which was rolled down on the stage, like a curtain when Damayanthi dies, it sheltered her body. It reminded Sudha of the temple tree that she had watched. It had sheltered Gods with minor defects that were discarded as unworthy of worship.

Some worship only the cross, with an absent Christ. Some worship only the head, with an absent body. Some worship only the snake, with an absent deity. I worship only a living tree, sheltering abandoned gods.

The group was travelling to Jaipur on a train from Bangalore. The journey was a long one. Sudha's parents trusted her to take care of herself. Her younger sister knew that Sudha was not happy. The theatre troupe was joyous travelling together, as usual as munching peanuts, cracking jokes, singing songs. Sudha was happy to be surrounded by laughter, but she was not in a mood to contribute to the merry-go-around as she plugged her ears with a Walkman and did not choose to listen to the teAsring. But Gopi and Rakshith wanted a sexual toy, the one available attractive toy was immersed in its own world, so they complained to Sachidanand who gently prodded her to open her ears to the life around. She really lacked the spirit to fight back.

They played Antakshari (a musical game of songs in which every player had to sing a song beginning with the last letter of the song of the previous player). It was fun when only one parameter of the letter was followed.

But Gopi and Rakshith began to read double meanings in all her songs, so she had to either lose the game by not singing a song with the right letter, but the wrong meaning or sing it and be misunderstood. This was worse than ragging; it was a collective determination to set her up with one of them either Gopi or Rakshith. Since most of the vernacular songs had 'Krishna' a synonym for Gopi, he was elated, as though he was the chosen one. So Sudha balanced one such song with another antonym song. But the effort depressed her, why would they not leave her alone?

She indirectly sought help from Samprada as she seemed to be neutral and did not make the rules. Samprada tactfully picked a bar of chocolate in her hand and made a show of giving it to Sudha. When she went to take it, Sampada playfully took it away, smiled and said, 'Don't do it to others.'

Sudha was sweet as a person and she did not know to be a bitch, so where were the tutorials held to be trained as a bitch?

Sudha wanted to tell her that she was not a tease. She really did not want to be in this game, she could not jump out of the train, and she did not know how to remain alone when someone made emotional demands. If she accepted it as just a simple game, they made it a sexual game, called her a tease. If she did not play then they would say she was reading too much into a simple game.

In that group members changed husbands, so what was the problem with boyfriends? A girl with a cunt had to have a partner, another sort of indoctrination. You could be gay, paedophile, necrophile, but you ought to love someone, they would not let you waste your youth. As though the most successful youth meant having sex with as many partners as possible.

Sudha tried to befriend Gopi trying to get some sense into his head, but her friendly gesture was seen as a move by all. The fact that she talked to him meant more than what she tried to say. And Gopi who needed an official girlfriend, behaved like a helium balloon, flying in the air. The older actors congratulating, what did they think? Such a band of cartoons, Sudha was cornered. No one bothered about the play or the story told in it, here people pretended for no reason, at best to pick up dates and socialize, not for any social change, which they spoke of in interviews. All the earnestness was a show, like the drama.

She wanted to enact the role of Amba, Damayanthi, and listen to those heart-wrenching songs, to enter a different world of a different time. The feminist theme explored by a woman, in a folk style, she was not here to socialize or pick up friends or boyfriends.

Though there was a gypsy lurking in her eyes, dancing in her toes. That was a tiny, wild molecule of her existence always checked by the larger wisdom of her person. She could release that gypsy only on stage where she belonged; this drama off the stage was draining the gypsy, releAsring the wisdom, wearily curtailing her talent.

Sudha slept that night in the train on her top berth, she would not sleep on the lower berth, and she feared being watched by those in the upper berths. She removed her teddy bear for comfort; she did not care for these jokers. Gopi was in a berth adjacent to her, he smiled tenderly looking at her Teddy, and he, fortunately, did not tease. But Sudha could not sleep at all, she could not toss fearing a fall, the distance between the top berth and the top of the train was very less. Whenever Sudha closed her eyes, she unpleasantly felt as if someone was bending over her, someone was on top of her, it terrified her. She liked open spaces, she trusted them.
When they reached Jaipur, it was evening. They checked in to a hotel, it was reasonably comfortable. Their play was scheduled to be held the next day, but they all decided to go watch the play scheduled for that evening enacted by a Bengali troupe.

The auditorium was huge with dark pink cotton screens, and side wings coloured saffron yellow. The huge brass lamp in the corner had a long strand of jasmines decorating its waist. There was a short length of flowers almost touching the flame. And a scene depicted that part of Mahabharath, where the Pandavas have fled from a palace of wax. They escaped a plot designed to kill them in the guise of a fire accident. So they disguise themselves and are serving in a palace of another king, as common servants. Draupadi is a hairdresser, Arjun is a eunuch and a dance teacher, Bheem is a cook.

So the choice of their roles was amazing, Draupadi whose only symbol of protest was her undone hair, was a hairdresser. An archer with deft fingers could also be a dancer. But a man as a dancer had to be a eunuch, how sexist! And Bheem an angry man, deeply in love with Draupadi, is also a cook. Reversal of tangible anger as edible food, a wave of very productive anger indeed! Chopping the vegetables, pealing the skin, grating them, boiling them, frying, steaming in a pressure cooker, adding spices, it must be therapeutic; to cook angrily she had seen her mother at it.

Then begins the sexual harassment of Draupadi by Keechak a lusty king, it caused agitation. One woman hounded repeatedly, why some women attracted abuse? This man Keechak did not know her history of being abused in an open court or polyandry or royalty, but he attempts to sexually abuse her. Was its beauty that she could not disguise? So hiding oneself to escape abuse how long would that work? Wasn't hiding in itself a form of self-abuse? Bheem finally kills Keechak; Arjun is convicted to the role of a eunuch. So, eunuch woman attains bravery but a eunuch man loses it. Femininity weakened a human more than the loss of sexuality, Sudha wanted to weep.

She left the auditorium in tears, she could not afford to break, and this place had strangers. All Gods were symbols of human frailties and strengths. Shiva beheaded his most intelligent son Ganesh, what would Freud say to that? Brahma married his own daughter, the most intelligent and docile goddess on the swan, so who was Electra? Freud/Jung spoke volumes about the complex emotion the child felt for father but no one bothered to illustrate what the father or mother felt in that situation. So what did god feel if he was human, no book spoke of that? The drama was a magnifying glass, selectively magnifying problems, dressing them up in royal costumes, solutions did not wear crowns, they could not be found on stage.

She did not see Gopi following her. She wanted to talk to her sister, go to a telephone booth. She was replacing her father with Sachidanand... every other older man, she was disloyal. She loved her father, but she could not express it, she was searching for him everywhere.

Gopi smiled vaguely, "You are very emotional, it was not a great presentation, I did not follow the Bengali words, not a word, and strange accent isn't it?" Sudha was silent, she had to suffer the attention of at least one man that was the rule, this man only talked and talked, so like her he was physically inhibited. He would not make a move physically, he had no peripheral vision. He only looked at her face; he would begin with the most difficult erogenous zone of her body that is her mind. He was stupid, and he did not know that he had no chance there. So if she needed a cover he was the safe bet. She looked at his innocent juvenile concern over her tears. He was comfortable with genuine pain, he was at ease with a girl, and maybe he lived with many women in the family, a matriarchy. Because there was no undue fascination, nor a need to dominate a woman, the moment a spark of attraction is felt. He trusted power in the feminine hands, it had nurtured him, and he had no ego hassles with women.

But he was a man; patriarchy safeguarded his interests, so in the long run, he would be a winner on both sides. He wanted a woman to dominate him and take care of him; he would not grow up soon.

Sudha was like a tattered doll. She needed first aid, she was looking for safety, that to the basic, physical safety, an asylum. She said simply, artlessly "I dislike Rakshith and his innuendos. Can you stop him?" the only safe number was one, not five. Gopi nodded like a protective deserving elder brother, handling a security assignment.

Sudha was assessing the risk abnormally, now she wanted neither, but eliminating both would unite them. She was hyper-vigilant, instinctually protecting herself. They went back to the hotel, the girls in her room were smoking, and it looked macho, kind of powerful statement. But doing all that men did would not empower a woman; so she tried to sleep in vain. The clouds of smoke wafting through her nostrils, infusing a sense of insecurity she always felt around men. The scene of Draupadi's abuse kept recurring in her mind; she could not replace it with another image. She needed her father, only with him she felt safe.

All her fears were imaginary, there were so many actors in the troupe, and no one could overpower her without her consent. If she sang or danced or spoke to a man, he could not jump on her and rape her. No harm could befall her in a public space. Just because some men were romantically interested did not mean anything would happen, but like the language of a dream, it had no logic. Then guilt recurred like a wave, it was associated with murderous rage towards a father and an equally strong desire to crawl into his lap. That sort of irrational rage towards the father made the loving child guilty. But the love caused a sense of disloyalty towards the mother, so love hurt, not loving hurt more.

The rehearsal in the theatre was conducted by Samprada in full gusto. Sachidaanand was doing the stagecraft, arranging the lights, props. He was a connoisseur; Samprada was an artist that was the stability in their association. He was gentle, she was crass, but they held on together. Sudha now knew that Sachidaanand's wife Khushi was a sort of an invalid, and he was the backbone of the organization 'Reaction' for years. They had weathered several mishaps together, they belonged together. They had jointly reared their daughters but the children disliked their stronger parents, preferring to sympathize with the absent parent. So they failed as parents of children, but their brainchild was with them, so was their bond.

Though Sudha had not yet seen the girls she was told all about them by other members. Sudha wanted to depend on Sachidaanand and not on Gopi. She feared with Gopi it may lead to romantic misinterpretations, but there was an invisible line of control around the older man, though he was the manager of the troupe and was supposed to resolve the interpersonal problems in group interaction.

Samprada was enacting the role of Madri. She was so self-preservative. Sudha would often wonder at the peaceful smile of reassignment in the dying face of Madri. Was that Khushi who was dying, sparing Sachidaanand at last to Samprada? As Sudha delivered her speech of begging for love to Salwa, she almost broke down twice. How many times she had to do this damn scene, how many times to steal herself, how many times to isolate her affect, pretend it was an actor when she was begging that invisible man miles away cozy in his connubial bliss actually, how to pretend a reality and call it a pretense? The man she had imagined as her perfect man with whom she had not exchanged anything more than few words was married to another woman. She had spoken of her interest in him too late…

It was tragic because she knew today she felt all this and never expressed any of it to that man, fearing rejection even before rejection, but she was still hurt by his rejection. Gopi was deeply disturbed by the reality which he sensed in her act, he would mechanically deliver his dialogues, when his whole self-wanted to pick her up, hold her and console her, and say 'Please don't cry, whatever it is that you are crying for is not worth this pain.' She could see that empathy pulsating across the stage as loudly as though he had screamed it, but it made no dent on her, she was inconsolable.

Then the scene with Bhishma enraged her sending her into a fury, she thundered, she was brilliant in anger. She never lost her senses in anger; she lost it only in love. After all, she had joined this troupe to voice anger. Then she self immolates, how many times should the universe suggest suicide, before she could actually do it? Why was she living on shamelessly, only symbolically entering fire on stage, that inner voice was chastising, 'Isn't this humiliation enough? Why are you still alive go die, go die, go die!'

Sudha was at war within herself, 'I have no right to take any one's life, even mine, that is violence, I will not be violent, it is sacrilege.' As the group surrounded her holding torches of flames, she was desperately resisting the urge to grab one of the torches and set herself ablaze, she really did not want to live without love, without God, angry with dance, music, her own soul. Angry with her father who had failed to protect her, even when she did not oppose patriarchy and submitted believing it was meant to protect a woman. He was not there when the worst happened...

After the show, the group seemed to be united, she felt left out of a conspiracy. Whenever she went to a toilet or to try some costume there were whispers, which became noise as soon as she was back. They were rejecting her, alienating her. But in actuality, they were worried sick. They were actors, they knew she was not performing an act on stage; she was living some unlived scenes of her life, suitably adapting their script to voice some profound anguish. They were emotional, sensitive men and women as all artists are. They did not know her at all, she hailed from a well to do a high profile, stable, family, what could devastate a girl from such a background it made no sense. Dramatists that they were they imagined matters to be far worse than the reality. Being an attractive young girl, it had to be that she was in love with some good for nothing creature, maybe her family had separated them; the only decent plausible explanation was that.

So the next day, Sachidaanand took her out alone for a coffee and confided in her about a Japanese girl he had courted and was forced to leave, how painful that was. He was actually in tears, reliving his first love story; Sudha gave him some Kleenex and was quiet. By then she was unable to reason her pain, she was numb. She could not speak, not completely understand what her reactions ought to be. She was travelling in a hazy reality, and nothing seemed real. She felt completely helpless, not quite all there. She merely mumbled that she was fine to Sachidaanand; all through the auto he confessed his million affairs, how horrid he was, Sudha was weary of confessions. It never consoled her to know others committed bigger crimes, it was her own gold standard for her, she was her own drummer, and she lived with her conscience, not someone else's. Men who confided their darkest secrets so easily would not treat her secrets with any sort of respect.

The last show was the story of the princess who brought rains. The director took a bold chance with her in the lead, as she usually performed despite her pathetic sadness. Sudha managed the first half of the play till she lost the gem with the power to bring rains, but the dance of grief she performed in real grief, and then she pretended to kill herself in front of the goddess. She had to lie like a corpse on the stage below the tree. That final step of the dance was to take twirls in clockwise and anti-clockwise directions, then fall dead under the tree. That was the trick to not disturb the semicircular canals of her ears and cause giddiness. Sudha wanted to sleep, she was tired. Here darkness was also safely magnified. On this stage no one looked after anyone, everyone looked on.

She felt strangely at home, on stage, under a cloth tree, in front of all audience. No one could rape her here, it was too open, too public, and everything done here was merely an act or a game, with no consequence so it was safe to sleep. She did not want to be resurrected anyway, so why to bother; she fell asleep. She had a beautiful dream... There was a dark forest, lit by angular sun rays intermittently. The road was familiar, winding, curving, a cool damp ground, she was walking bare feet like inside a temple. She was not alone, someone else was breathing, quite near, as though the other person and she were locked in a tight embrace, but she could not see the face. Everything was bound to be dark at that close distance, there was no light, she needed the sun. There was a distinct smell to this man, it reminded her of some deeply buried, only half-remembered intimacy of some other life, either below the sea, or above the sky, or at the core of the earth, unseen, unheard, untouched, just a smell.

They woke her up, she had slept through the scenes of the resurrection of the princess after the gem is brought by the prince. It had caused huge embarrassment on stage when she did not wake up with polite cues, Samprada had taken over the role... Only after the curtains were drawn, and she had been shaken awake.

She saw that the play was over; she just got up and accompanied them to the green room. Someone helped her with the removal of the makeup, she changed her costumes alone, and she did not want help. Unlike the other girls, Sudha would not change her clothes even in front of a girl. There was a theatre actor, who was also a psychiatrist. He knew Samprada, and so they wanted him to talk to her in the silent, dark auditorium, emptied of its audience. He introduced himself sitting next to her; she was too tired to open up to a stranger, or to anyone. It was too long a story, spanning from the age of seven. What was the use of telling anyway, it would resemble everyone's story, just another story with some different names substituting the original? The only original element was a pain, and it could not be shared, so why bother to waste her breath.

"Can you tell me what is upsetting you? Do you need help?" At least this man was a professional, unlike silly sweet Sachidaanand he did not tell her "Listen, child, I have slept with sixteen thousand women, so you can trust me." Sudha spoke in a clear voice, his hushed tone as though it was okay for her to confess that she had just murdered her father irritated her. "Sir, I have been depressed lately and consulted Dr. Kannur, but he wanted my depression to mature, only then he could treat it he said, sort of like cataract or something. For melodramatic satisfaction, I can tell you one man broke my heart, another man my hymen, so I am in this state, like a stupor, whether it is the depressive or dissociative state I don't know!" He was a better actor than a doctor, he looked calm.

"So you rather want Dr. Kannur to treat you, is that what you are saying?" "Yes, once I choose a doctor, I seldom change. I don't like doctor shopping; we can change the doctor, not the disease, is it not?" He smiled at her persuasive talk, "Your group was very concerned, they say you are having a breakdown, you were fine when you boarded the train, but gradually within forty-eight hours this has happened."

"Everything inside me is broken, so it is a breakdown I suppose." Sudha's voice was hoarse. He stared thoughtfully; he did not want to medicate her. Sudha was worried what if she had said too much, what if he told it all to everyone? "Sir, I hope you will maintain confidentiality, you can tell the disease, not other personal details." He understood that he nodded. Later that night Sudha was taken to one room with Samprada and Sachidaanand. There were two cots, Sudha had to sleep with Samprada in one cot, and Sachidaanand slept in the other cot. This arrangement was made to ensure that Sudha was protected and observed at the same time, the doctors always saw sanity, and artists saw her vulnerability.

Both thought finally she was a fraud, she felt guilty of a crime she did not commit. Her intelligence was deceptively orderly. Amidst artists it permitted indulgence, with doctors only rationale. There was very little spillover, there was a near-total dichotomization, almost as if she were two distinct persons, though both were aware of the other. Sudha woke up after some time, she asked Samprada to go sleep with Sachidaanand, and she did not want to come between them. She loved them both equally. Mother and father should sleep on one cot, only then the child could be free.

She requested repeatedly, but to no avail. An open secret was still a secret. Samprada was obviously scandalized; she concluded Sudha was raving mad. Sudha spent one more sleepless night, she went for a morning walk with Sachidaanand, unsolicited, and she did not want to be alone with Samprada... she did not want to murder Bhishma.

So she was taken to meet the actor psychiatrist again, there the man dialled her house. When Sudha heard her sister's voice on the phone, she wept, "I am not a good sister, I am not good enough, I am not protecting you or taking care of you as I should." Meenu was concerned, she gave the phone to her dad. He sounded very afraid, she could hear the fear of insanity inspired in dear ones. Out of body experiences were experienced in a body, out of mind was felt by a mind, insanity was merely another state of mind, that a common man mystified and feared.

Sudha did not mystify mental illness. Like the ghost of her brother she must have some of his qualities, and she would never fear it, would probably love it as much. The insane version of a person was as yet one of his versions, it was him not an alien. She was hurt 'I am okay daddy, just feeling blue that is all, everyone is overreacting.' Samprada spoke to her dad, Sudha could not concentrate on their conversation.

She was given antipsychotic, quite a strong dose. They did not want her running around in the train or jumping off the train. Sudha crashed in the train into a drugged sleep. They forced her to eat in between. Gopi was trying to talk to her. Now Sudha was so confused by these drugs, the only two thoughts in her mind were she was on a train; her mind was reversing the clock, like a rewind button, regressing the milestones, to a train journey long ago. Now she looked at Gopi drowsily, "Can I hold your hand?" Then he held her hand and she fell asleep, she was knocked out of her senses by these drugs.

So the hand remained firmly in her grasp, did the idol of God contain the God? Was it just a symbol? It would become a dwelling of the divine, if one prayed sincerely, even for one minute. Faith had that quality of timelessness. So in her death-like drugged sleep, Damayanthi had conquered a broken prince, he wanted to resuscitate her, somehow, anyhow, at any cost. She wanted to fold her hands like sleeves, her fingers were cold, numb, and she was sinking in a whirlpool. She had to die, die, die, but a hand was not letting her go. It tugged her hand hurting her, "Come out, pull, pull, you can make it, you have to live!" The voice did not belong to the owner of the hand, the voice had entered some hand, she had to retrieve the will to live. Like how she ran across the shore of the swimming pool screaming at her little sister, "You have to win, you have to pull, you can, you can, do it!"

She could not abandon herself; her god was everywhere, in every human being who watched her in that train, every pair of eyes looking over her. She could not die in the public eye, and death was a private experience. Besides, they had paralyzed her motor system, with neuroleptic drugs, no hope of playing Anna

Karenina. She could only feel the movement around, she was asleep she could not move, like when the rapist was on top of her she could not move. She was reliving her dream, she could not eat, she had forgotten how. The train rocked like a cradle, the hand-pulled, was it her moving the train? She only longed for the permanent, she wanted permanent sleep.

But life beckoned her, luring her like the breeze of the summer, like the glow of a single candle, like the tune of the single flute, like the single tooth of a baby smile, like the single mole on her mother's upturned chin, like the single dimple of her father's reluctant smile. Life seduced her like her own swaying hips, like the trembling sweaty hands holding her waist, like her electrifying dancing feet, like the kiss of a male mouth-melting her, like the maddening unintentional glimpse of her cleavage. When they reached Bangalore, Samprada and Sachidaanand took her home. Sudha did not recall anything of that train journey, except for holding Gopi's hand. In the broad daylight, getting closer to her house, looking at the faces of these two artists, nervously taking unspoken partial responsibility for her madness, she felt the enormity of her behaviour. Maybe the neuroleptic numbing her nervous system quietened her dopamine, and increased the prolactin, improving her bonding strategies. Her father opened the door, invited Samprada and Sachidaanand inside. They sat around stiffly making inane remarks, and they could not speak of her 'breakdown' in front of her. So she facilitated their polite discussions and went to her room.

Her poems were scattered, all her books were opened read, even her diary was not spared. All her anonymous gifts were probed for their hidden meanings, like a cyclone in her room, the disorder hurt. They did not even care to rearrange it before she came, they did not want her to have a shred of privacy. How many editions of human rights translations were required? She slept like an injured butterfly, metamorphosis hurt more than the indolent cocoon. She would live like a worm, anaemic caterpillar with less hair. How dare she desire the colour on her face or a crown or a veil? She could not think, the drug was making her drowsy again. She slept the whole day, waking up by evening. Her mother came to the room, and Sudha ate the food given to her like a prisoner, jailed for some unproven crime. After all unproved innocence is also an unproven crime.

No one asked her a simple direct question 'What happened?' So she did not think of the answer.

~***~

8. fame

~~~~~~~~~~~~~~~~~~~***~~~~~~~~~~~~~~~~

After a few weeks, Sudha went to the theatre meetings again. Now she felt she had to enact that role on stage once successfully, to overcome the feeling implied in it. She did not want the set up to affect her responses anymore, it was just a role. If she could always not stop herself from identifying with the victim, she would be a victim always, suicide was not an option. But the process was tedious; she had to encounter all her ghosts.

Initially, there was awkwardness, but Samprada was extremely kind, she had solved the mystery behind Sudha's need to be on stage. When stage, as a space was needed by someone, Samprada understood, she had inherited that need. The need was not necessarily fame; it was simply to be oneself or to rise above the self. Even if it caused her to go mad, she wanted it. That was her passion, and Samprada's entire being melted for that.

The sleep on stage, under the tree and insomnia in bed inside the room, beside her, a child begging the mother and father to sleep together, unable to sleep, unless they did, strangely touched Samprada. She had finally seen the break of discipline, loss of self-control, in Sudha and realized with a shock, like how control made her insane. Lack of control made Sudha insane, so it was not hypocrisy; it was her form, her shape, her irrefutable mold. This anger, unbridled passion that was Samprada's
~~~~~~~~~~~~~~~~~~~

pulse, breath, baseline, was an alien frequency for Sudha. What was effortless for Samprada was a steep hill for Sudha. But now Sudha was wiser, she knew her limit, besides, there was an inexplicable sympathy towards the unfair gender. Her father could not voice his concern, but though silent concern was there. He had wept over her distress. Though her privacy was not respected, it was human to worry. Though the surface was not believed, it was wise to know the depth. Her love was always reciprocated, so was her hate. Then how can her faith built on these be futile?

She knew that father was a man, but also human. She had seen his hands tremble when she spoke of the trauma. He was tormented; it broke him as much as it broke her. That tenderness in his occasional gaze when she looked happy and pretty moved her. He did not blame her, nor did he unduly pity her, he did monitor her whereabouts a little more than before. He needed to know where she was at any time during the day that was all. He did not censor her calls nor ask her uncomfortable questions. The confidence was respected. Her father did not suggest any specific mode of response, he felt for her, she was not alone, that was exactly what she needed.

At first everyone, in the troupe behaved as though nothing was amiss, the effort showed. There was a little more of pity, a little less respect, little bit of skepticism towards her cheerful attitude.

Sudha suffered silently. Gopi was affected by that clasp of her hand; it thoroughly embarrassed her to meet his eyes. She was irrepressibly miserable that drowsy night in the train, to ask him to hold her hand, she just ignored him, and he waited for her to look, to speak, to acknowledge that intimacy between them. She was unwilling to do that. The rehearsal, regular jokes, continued…. Sudha stayed out like a requiem or a dead starfish on the shore covered by sands, or ashes of thousand unwanted lovers. Gopi started to observe silence, not allowing her solitary world of soundlessness. This sharing of her silence was also intrusive, he was mighty stubborn, like a bull he demanded a friendship, her mere presence meant she was also interested.

Sudha knew whenever something crept up on her, it would not linger, she trusted her instincts. This man made her feel safe, but her pulse did not race; there was no spark or ignition here. It was sober, steady, almost like the way it is with a sibling. She really wanted a friend there, but this man wanted her, all of her. To pretend to not understand, be insensitive enough to call it fraternal, that was unpermitted in her ethics. But a certain tension built up when feelings were silently exchanged, without consent and were not verbalized. Words defined feelings strangely limiting them, but nonverbal feelings could give an illusion of profundity, a hint of a possibility which was impossible. Sudha now delivered Amba's dialogues not succumbing to the vulnerability or glorified self-pity but retaining the pathos, concentrating on voice modulation, not the feeling. When she left the rehearsal at night, he seemed lost, as though it hurt him to see her go away every night. He needed that feeling which she had unwittingly inspired, it pressurized her.

Samprada wanted to stage the same plays in Hampi an ancient city, once the capital of Hoysala dynasty, full of ruined, restored temples, a historic monument. Sudha was eager to go and perform, to overcome that fear of losing control about the loss of that gem to usher the rains. Imaginary losses could be recovered only in imagination, to search for them in reality, mourning that loss, in reality, was madness. What was really lost was just a nictitating membrane, she could not reset the clock, she could not go back in time to recover, and it was stripped off her.

Father did not stop Sudha. He knew when defeated, she was unperturbed by persuasion. She was stronger than when she went to Jaipur, at least one man knew the truth or the version of truth she could decipher then. He cried her tears, he did not understand what it meant for a woman, but she understood what it meant to have a father. Sudha entered the compartment of the theatre troupe at about the middle of the journey. This time there was no Rakshith, that role was done by someone else. But Gopi seemed to resent her self-reliance, it deleted him.

So he started the flirtation, chiding her spurious vulnerability, her suspect 'break down'. For Sudha, it was Déjà vu. The kindness, charm, delight of a human company when there is a sexual possibility quickly turning to mad rage, paranoia, and a compulsion to defame or slander the unavailable sexual object.

Mustering a nonexistent courage, dispensing all formalities, Sudha started the personal talk, "I am shit scared of going on stage and falling asleep, you know?" Gopi was thrown, "Why, you seem okay actually, you are good as an actor." Sudha continued, "That is where the problem arises, I become the role, then I am unable to switch off. I continue to be dead Damayanthi off stage or a raving eunuch in search of Bhishma, who was not killed on stage." He laughed, he was not Rakshith, and he did not guess the pathos.

He was vaguely embarrassed by the allusion to 'eunuch', so was he a puritan? He was sort of Victorian, disliked alluding to sex as a possibility. She had no intention to re-invite that talk about her break down, so she changed the topic. "So, who do you live with? I mean what do your parents do? Are you serious about acting? Will you pursue it as a profession?" He was silent for a while; family concealed some vulnerability, what was that? It seemed she had once again peeled a bandage, over an invisible wound. She stammered, "Did I ask something wrong?" He was eager to please, to keep the interest,

"No, No! My father is in the police department, Alur branch. I have a younger sister, a mother at home. My mother was interested in acting once upon a time. Although I studied law, I am interested to pursue acting."

But he spoke of his dad and mom as though they were separate units, it was implied, she was confused. "How do you intend to pursue acting, if the stage is your passion, NSD is where you must go, I guess, it will get you big openings, a platform to connect with the best minds in this field. Right?" He was sweetly unassuming, "It is not so easy Sudha, to get in. He asked her, "What do you want to do? Do you prefer to be an actor?" Sudha was clear, "Acting is just a hobby; I have no ambition in this." So they chatted for some time. He was a gentle companion, a clown in society, but when singled out he was morose, insecure, badly needing affection, almost as much as her. So she could be in control of this friendship, her instincts were right, he would never overstep his boundaries, there would be no violation here, this was safe. There was a mild air of ridicule, as though there was a romance brewing in the train, between them, but Sudha did not feel it. This friendship was her need to survive this setup, an umbrella in the rain.

So she chose to ignore the comments, the friendship would dilute the romance she thought. He thought it was the first step of an aisle; he was raw enough for ambition, tender enough to fall in love. Sudha was beyond the illusion of love, still caught in the recycling of revenge, passion reversed. Now marriage was merely an institution to rear children, a sort of temporary voluntary retirement from life, till the last child went to school, she did not believe in love. Commitment, loyalty, many such lofty replacements could enter that institution, but that racing of the pulse, speaking eyes, breaking voice, crying poetry was deleted. She could not live with that humiliation, called love.

God was a power, impersonal, a sort of law like gravitation, wisdom like integral calculus, cold like the metals in which he was made.

But after this talk, there was a thirst for more, to know more, to share more, and pleasantly warm. He seemed to be willing to say yes to anything, he had no defenses at all, it surprised her. She was used to the generally defensive, *'I know more than thou' 'Yikes, Actress, I am holier than thou'* or *'Show me some attitude, where are those sexy legs, why can't we make out in the car?'*

Here there was no pressure, no expectations; he wanted them to hang around together, talk, talk that is all. She liked him immensely. So he even accompanied her to the cobbler as the strap of her platform heels tore, in the middle of a sightseeing trip to a ruined temple of Veerupaksha. He laughed at the size of her heels; he did not know it was purchased to look taller to dwarfs with equal height. She dragged her foot with the torn strap, like a graceful sleepy dance stride, she would not walk bare feet. She said, "The heavy heels are to keep me held to the ground, facilitating the gravitational pull.' He was amused, "You can't be simple at all, about anything, can you? You seem to be lost somewhere in the sky, and talk of gravitation, etc." So it was like that with them, she could talk, blabber anything, he would dote on her. Now there was no power struggle between them. For Sudha that dimension would not arise unless the other person introduced it. The defiance instigated by authority, hence the need to neutralize the power by endless games was missing.

So they were happy like children, backstage, helping each other with the cardboard crowns. This time she enjoyed the pretending, butterflies in the stomach before the raise of the curtains, looks of appreciation when some costume suited her, shy prompting, and exaggerated chivalrous cues for her lines.

There were private hints like a camouflaged wink when she cried over Salwa's refusal to marry her, reminding her it was an act, not letting her drown in the mask, and borrow the colours of the mask into her face. The change of costumes backstage at an urgent speed, a flurry of feet, thumbs up when every fragment was in place, the nervous giggles, over someone else's mistake, surprise at some one's overacting, the general fun of teamwork. Backstage, green room, even the stage was pathetically ill-equipped, with all the poverty of capital of bygone days, not at all like the modern cum ethnic décor of Jaipur theatre stage.

While jumping from the backstage which was just a table of joined wooden benches, hence shaking violently with their jumps, Gopi extended his hand, for Sudha to hold, but he made her feel that she was holding his hand again, as though she was waiting for her turn, it insulted her. Because it reminded her of helpless, drugged state, in that train, he had misunderstood that gesture; it was a response to some frantic, imaginary fear. Though the danger was imaginary, the terror was real, how to explain, without revealing the shameful secret, she did not know.

Samprada was growing possessive of Gopi, strangely protective towards him, as though he was being misused, such confusing signals. Sudha did not understand her at all. In some picturesque locales of the ruins, Gopi wanted her photographs, mentioning that he would show them to his mother. Sudha was afraid of his genuine intentions. Her feelings for Gopi were not that of romantic love, it would be self-deception, to comply.

So again, she was in a quandary, on the way back, to Bangalore she decided to talk about Jaipur. Though she could not talk about real trauma, she did not know him well enough, but she could tell him about some man she had imagined to be her love to realize he was already committed to somebody else and she did not want Gopi on the rebound. Her feelings at this stage could not be trusted. But that had the undesired effect of making him see her as the kind of woman who was capable of falling madly in love, which was attractive in itself. Besides if she could love someone with whom she had no actual relationship at all, it licensed him to love a woman who said she did not love him at all.

Receiving such strong feelings for free, unnerved her, making her guilty, as though she had maneuvered it somehow. He spoke of how he had held her hand all through the night in the train, despite the numbness. How he was worried about her for days, searching for her house in the neighborhood, all sorts of theories about her madness which he had concocted in his head, trying to come up with the least harmful. She was touched, she was sorry; she had affected him like this. Why did she decompensate so acutely, completely she did not know. Now after two months she was not at all scared, though mood swings continued. She did feel sadder than she had felt before. Each time she thought it can't get worse, but the next bout was worse. They reached Bangalore; she did feel the pang the end of a happy holiday usually caused her. She had given him her telephone number, taken his office number; they were going to be in touch.

He loved her, it was there for everyone to see, she was using his feelings to heal herself, she was being thoroughly selfish, dishonest, and felt ashamed.

Just as she reached home, he called her. He wanted to hear her voice. She laughed into the phone, and she needed this spoiling, many years since she had experienced this kind of longing for her in a man. She really wished she could love him, but that feeling was not under the control of a will, not even her indomitable will. Sudha met Samprada's daughter Karishma in one of the theatre meetings. Karishma was a good friend of Gopi, so she was curious about Sudha. This girl lived in a world where the only rule was *'Hate your parents, all else would be pardoned.'* She was living the kind of life devoid of hypocrisy, led by her impulses, smoking continuously, changing husbands, suicide attempts, utter chaos. Samprada's irreverence for self-control personified.

But Karishma started to tell Sudha that the theatre group thought of Sudha as a mentally ill person. They joked about her madness behind her, etc. This upset Sudha, she became hypersensitive to all comments in the group. So she started avoiding the meetings, rejection either by an individual or by a group was too much to bear. When the relationship between two persons could hurt, to love a group and survive, Sudha could not.

But she and Gopi were friends, they spoke over the phone, they met in public places which Sudha suggested, so a Sharada temple, an amusement park, a library, a movie theatre, these were the spots she chose. Sudha shared her poems with him. He was protective, orthodox, and puritanical. He worshipped a woman, but strangely, it did not empower her, she felt like a fraud and as though she had no right to imperfections. But he Xeroxed her poetry, walked around with her photographs and poems in his bag.

They once watched a popular film, where all the love begins in a train, Sudha impulsively held his hand in the theatre, surprising him. The complete absence of a physical attraction was why Sudha felt it was not love, all other ingredients were present. That attraction, a tiny spark, a twitch, a sob, a touch of madness that was absent. She may never find it ever again, it frightened her like death, it was a lost gem, like her anger which had no target, and this love had no claimant, so it remained with her like a fragrance, whose origin was an enigma. She had to give up on that dream, to believe in the unknown, loyalty to absence was not faith but madness.

Gopi confided that his parents were divorced, his father had remarried. He remained with his mother and sister, he did not blame his father for the split, there was a silent accuse towards mother. He longed for his father; the sense of abandonment he felt was poignant.

Sudha realized why he constantly seemed like a little boy in a blue uniform with a tie, coming home to a lonely mother, being a clown to make her laugh and say in his own little charming ways, 'It does not matter if father left, he would have taken me, but I stayed back with you, I am a good son, is it not?' She knew how utterly shattered a child must feel to hear his parents declare in an open court that they no longer love each other, to choose one parent over another, to feel angry with the one who had custody, to feel guilty towards the one who walked away, to begin a life knowing that love ends.

Naturally, he was attracted to strong women who seemed to be in conflict with their social unit. He could be there for such a woman, and it had become a habit. The woman would be a demigod; he would surrender, to be taken care of by her. Sudha was not up to it, she was equally immature, she also wanted a demigod to take care of her, and she did not wish to grow up at all, so even emotionally they were unsuited to each other.

She would visit the infant Jesus church in Viveknagar, sometimes early mornings, or late evenings. She would derive some peace, strength and more loneliness, a sort of aimlessness by these visits. Hate gave her a focus in the absence of love, so when she let go of that hate, it caused a frightening emptiness, lethargy, fatigue. Gopi came with her once to this church, since they both loved the father, and were thwarted in their expression of that love; they shared this love of God, and quest for father figures.

But Sudha was conditioned to believe, to fear, to expect, her intellect worked at loggerheads with her feelings. She believed those who believed in God, at least they still retained hope of universal order. The hopelessness inherent in the murder of God, any god chilled her. Gopi would sit silently watching her pray, talk to God, alone in the church, often in tears, he did not understand. He did not question patriarchy, even though his father left his mother, because of patriarchy. Gopi had sheltered her by virtue of his gender, so it empowered him, though it was the mother who had nurtured him, and empowered him, considering he was only nine years old when his father left.

So like Salwa, he drove her to look for a father figure, he would not partake in her problems with authority or power. He had chosen the easy path, to befriend that power, to survive. He had chosen to stay with mother in an open court, he had defied father, attempted to repair his mistake, even as a child, so the power of the father did not scare him, it merely endeared. He had been an adult as a child, he had been a miniature father aged all of nine years. He was used to loving a strong woman, without possessing her sexually, but to duplicate that in matrimony would be a gross injustice, Sudha would not be guilty of that crime.

Sudha accompanied him to his bachelor quarters one fine day. After several meetings in public, she trusted him. He was kind, sensitive, so completely in love with her; she wanted to come for his sake. He had decorated his humble room, tastefully for her sake, the beauty was in the effort. There was a stuffed fluffy colorful parrot, made of woolen cloth, battery-operated, repeating all that she said, it was so childish like her, she cried and put her head on his shoulder. He hugged her, hesitantly, tried an inexperienced kiss. She realized this would never lead them anywhere, she could not reciprocate. It was self-deception to continue, his pride was tender, it was his first love, she did not wish to destroy his confidence, but it was all wrong. She was numb.

She did not know how to tell a man at this stage that she did not love him, she tried. She felt truly awful that was the end of private meetings, they could not proceed beyond the kiss, she was not going to pretend with him, she owed him that much.

Their play was on stage, not off stage. A man who had let her walk all over him like a strong Teddy bear, like forgiving mother earth, to facilitate her drama, deserved the truth. He may forgive her for using him some distant day, but she would not forgive herself if she let him think she loved him, the imagined lover was long dead in her mind, but she would blame him or anyone but she could not continue this misunderstood romantic liaison. Not all debts could be repaid. This man deserved a woman who would love him; he would find her, only if she left. So Sudha was determined to leave.

Sudha saw that the theatre form was giving way to the small screen, actors on stage, were thronging the television producer's offices for roles her interests were dwindling. But the show-biz did not charm Sudha any more, it did not matter whether someone looked at her or not, whether someone thought of her as pretty or smart or talented. She had seen the way Gopi had shown her off to his dad as though she was a trophy; he wanted fame…

Fame was longing for his name to become bigger than his father whose name he only carried on paper. A sort of veiled revenge, 'You walked out on us, but I made you famous, you will be known as my dad, I don't need your name.' The orphan adopting the name of his skill, his art, his science, his God, in turn, adopted by the world. The identity that could not be inherited was earned by the child. Sometimes fame was the only royal road to be acknowledged by that one father as his child. The whole world may appreciate but until that one man acknowledged it was incomplete.

In women it was the defiance towards the surname, husband or father it did not matter, to not to be defined or limited by that one relationship, hence aching to bond with the whole world. To avenge a mother dominated by patriarchy. But there was a longing to make up for some loss the parent had endured. Sometimes it was a legacy, the holy mission of carrying the family name.

This hunger for fame had at its root a sort of shame, a namelessness, and identity crisis reminiscent of adolescence. It was the definition of 'me' as bigger than what produced me, a brief kiss of immortality. A shadow reproduced a thousand times, even after the death of the veteran. Cinema was a medium where the shadow grew bigger than the person himself, annihilating the father.

So Gopi had plenty of inspiration, he needed a ladder. Sudha was disenchanted with fame; to her, it contained an invisible price tag, a series of private humiliations, masked by a public name, so she did not care. She loved her father, she only abhorred patriarchy, a system which victimized him too and she could not even annihilate her private patriarch on stage for a drama. So to her fame and name were mere addresses of a person. Innocence, love, a gem to bring rains, she needed to find it. So their meeting was bound to end at these crossroads.

~***~

www.ingramcontent.com/pod-product-compliance
Lightning Source LLC
La Vergne TN
LVHW040218180726
843492LV00011B/158